MW01134495

Living Books Press

# Aesop's Fables

with

## Scripture References

Compiled and Edited by
Sheila Carroll

Introduction by
G.K. Chesterton

Fable text translation by
V.S. Vernon Jones

Illustrations by
Arthur Rackham

Living Books Press™
Mount Pleasant, Michigan

The fable text was translated from the original Greek by V.S. Vernon Jones and first published in 1912 by Doubleday, Page; Heinemann, New York; London. The illustrations are from the same edition by the English illustrator Arthur Rackham (1867-1939).

The Living Books Press edition has edited the fables and arranged them alphabetically for easy reference. Additionally, the LBP edition has added Scripture references, study and application notes, and a glossary of terms.

LIVING BOOKS PRESS™
Publishers of classic *living* books
5497 Gilmore Road
Mt. Pleasant, Michigan 48858
www.livingbookscurriculum.com



Design and prepress by
Carrousel Graphics, Jackson, Wyoming

ISBN: 0-9790876-7-8
ISBN-13: 978-0-9790876-7-7

Printed in the United States of America.

Preface to the 2007 Edition

# The Excellency of a Fable

> This indeed is the exellency of the fable, that it conveys advice without the appearance of doing so.
>
> Rev. George Fyler Townsend,
> Preface to *The Fables of Aesop*

Teaching with fables is an ancient tradition found in every culture. Fables are — and were meant to be — for everyone. Children benefit from them because their young minds are still forming, and adults benefit from them because as adults we continue to mature.

The *Aesopic* fable as a literary form has a special place in world literature. Its form is an elegantly terse story which expresses a basic truth. Apollonius of Tyana, a first century A.D. philosopher, said of Aesop:

> "...like those who dine well off the plainest dishes, he made use of humble incidents to teach great truths, and after serving up a story he adds to it the advice to do a thing or not to do it."[1]

Texts of Aesop's fables have a long and honorable tradition in publishing history. It is thought that Aesop gathered from oral tradition and also composed hundreds of his own fables. Later another Greek, Barbrius, collected, organized, and recorded what became known as Aesop's Fables. Manuscripts were hand-copied; new translations made. Across the classical world the fables were included in books of poetry, plays, speeches, and essays as illustrations of the writer's point. Socrates, according to his biographer Aristotle, composed couplets from the fables as he awaited execution.

After the fall of Rome, most manuscripts were lost. However, those that were saved were held in the libraries of Byzantine scholars. Much later, during the Renaissance, Greek learning was revived, and the fables came into general favor once again. Scholars and teachers of that period translated them from the original Latin and Greek. The invention of the printing press by Johann Gutenberg in 1436, made possible multiple copies of a single version. The fables spread across Europe. After the Bible, the fables were among the most reproduced books.

Martin Luther, a trained classical scholar, was partial to fables and translated many from the original Latin:

> "Aesop lay on the same table with the Book of Psalms, and the two translations proceeded alternately. Except for the Bible, he declared the he knew no better book, and pronounced it not to be the work of any single author but the fruit of the labours of the greatest minds of the ages."[2]

As an educator long familiar with Aesop's fables, I had not expected to learn more when working on this edition. I am pleased to say I was quite wrong. Again and again I was struck with the fables' deep wisdom, humor, and insight into the workings of the human heart. I learned from these ancient tales. Then, when I set them against the light of Scripture, I found each the brighter for the comparison. It is my prayer you will too.

We have made every effort to craft this edition for ease of use for family Bible study, homeschooling, Sunday school, and the general reader. *The Living Books Press Aesop's Fables* edition is a republication of the original 1912 edition, translated by V. S. Vernon Jones. It has been carefully edited to provide the reader a simple means of finding, reading, and studying the fables. Each moral has Scripture references and examples from biblical history to lend greater insight and understanding. The reader will find a complete glossary of unfamiliar words, an alphabetical listing of morals, a biography of Aesop, and a guide to further study that helps to enjoy the fables and learn from them again and again.

Sheila Carroll
Mount Pleasant, Michigan

---

(Endnotes)
1 Philostratus: *The Life of Apollonius of Tyana*, ed. Christopher P. Jones,
2 Stephen, James: *Essays in Ecclesiastical Biography*

# G.K. Chesterton Introduction

Aesop embodies an **epigram** not uncommon in human history: his fame is all the more deserved because he never deserved it. The firm foundations of common sense, the shrewd shots at uncommon sense, that characterise all the **fables** belong not only to him but to humanity. In the earliest human history whatever is authentic is universal: and whatever is universal is anonymous. In such cases there is always some central man who had first the trouble of collecting the stories, and afterwards the fame of creating them. He had the fame and, on the whole, he earned the fame. There must have been something great and human, something of the human future and the human past, in such a man: even if he only used it to rob the past or deceive the future.

For example, the legends of King Arthur and his Knights of the Roundtable may have been extracted from chronicles of the fighting for Christianity during the Crusades, and the eventual fall of Rome; or the story may have been born from the most heathen of traditions in the hills of Wales—the Celtic fairy tales. But the word "**Mappe**" or "**Malory**" will always mean King Arthur; even though we find older and better origins than the **Mabinogian**; or later and worse versions than the "Idylls of the King."

The nursery fairy tales may have come out of Asia with the Indo-European race, now fortunately extinct. These stories may have been invented by some fine French lady or gentleman like **Perrault**: they may possibly even be what they profess to be. But we shall always call the best selection of such tales "**Grimm's Tales**": simply because it is the best collection.

The historical Aesop, in so far as he was historical, would seem to have been a **Phrygian** slave. He lived, if he did live, about the sixth century before Christ, in the time of **Croesus** (whose story we love and hold in suspect, like everything else in **Herodotus)**. There are also stories of human deformity and a ready ribaldry of tongue: stories which (as the celebrated Cardinal said) explain, though they do not excuse, why Aesop was hurled over a high precipice at Delphi. It is for those who read the **Fables** to judge whether he was really thrown over the cliff for being ugly and offensive (or rather for being highly moral and correct). But there is little doubt that the general legend of Aesop may justly rank him with a race too easily forgotten in our modern comparisons: the race of the great philosophic slaves. Aesop may have been a fictional composite like **Uncle Remus**. He was also, like Uncle Remus, a fact. It is a fact that slaves in the old world could be worshipped like Aesop, or loved like Uncle Remus. It is odd to note that both the great slaves told their best stories about beasts and birds.

Whatever writings be credited to Aesop, the human tradition called fable was not his alone. This story form had gone on long before any sarcastic freedman from Phrygia had or had not been flung off a precipice; and has remained long after. It is to our advantage, indeed, to realise the distinction; because it makes Aesop more obviously effective than any other fabulist.

*Grimm's Tales*, glorious as they are, were collected by two German students. If we find it hard to be certain of German students, at least we know more about them than we know about a Phrygian slave. The truth is, of course, that *Aesop's Fables* are not Aesop's fables, any more than *Grimm's Fairy Tales* are Grimm's fairy tales. But the fable and the fairy tale are things utterly distinct. There are many elements of difference; but the plainest is plain enough. There can be no good fable with human beings in it. There can be no good fairy tale without them.

Aesop, or **Babrius** (or whatever his name was), understood that for a fable all the persons must be impersonal. They must be like abstractions in algebra, or like pieces in chess. The lion must always be stronger than the wolf, just as four is always double of two. The fox in a fable must move crooked, as the knight in chess must move crooked. The sheep in a fable must march on, as the pawn in chess must march on. The fable must not allow for the crooked captures of the pawn; it must not allow for what **Balzac** called "the revolt of a sheep".

The fairy tale, on the other hand, absolutely revolves on the pivot of human personality. If no hero is there to fight the dragons, we should not even know that they are dragons. If no adventurer is cast on the undiscovered island, it would have remained undiscovered. If the **miller's** third son does not find the enchanted garden where the seven princesses stand white and frozen—why, then, they will remain white and frozen and enchanted. If there is no personal prince to find the Sleeping Beauty she will simply sleep.

Fables repose upon quite the opposite idea: that everything is itself, and will in any case speak for itself. The wolf will be always wolfish; the fox will be always foxy. Something of the same sort may have been meant by the animal worship, in which Egyptian and Indian and many other great peoples have combined. Men do not, I think, love beetles or cats or crocodiles with a wholly personal love; they salute them as expressions of that abstract and anonymous energy in nature which to any one is awful, and to an atheist must be frightful. So in all fables (that are or are not Aesop's) all the animal forces drive like inanimate forces, like great rivers or growing trees. It is the limit and the loss of all such things that they cannot be anything but themselves: it is their tragedy that they could not lose their souls.

This is the immortal justification of the Fable: that we could not teach the plainest truths so simply without turning men into chessmen. We cannot talk of such simple things without using animals that do not talk at all. Suppose, for a moment, that you turn the wolf into a wolfish baron, or the fox into a foxy diplomatist. You will at once remember that even barons are human, you will be unable to forget that diplomatists are men. You will always be looking for that accidental good-humour that should go with the brutality of any brutal man; for that allowance for all delicate things, including virtue, that should exist in any good diplomatist. Once the writer puts a thing on two legs instead of four and plucks it of feathers, you cannot help asking for a human being, either heroic, as in the fairy tales, or un-heroic, as in the modern novels.

But by using animals in this austere and arbitrary style as they are used on the shields of heraldry or the hieroglyphics of the ancients, men have really succeeded in handing down those tremendous truths that are called truisms. If the chivalric lion be red and rampant, it is rigidly red and rampant; if the sacred ibis stands anywhere on one leg, it stands on one leg for ever. In this language, like a large animal alphabet, are written some of the first philosophic certainties of men.

As the child learns A for Ass or B for Bull or C for Cow, so man has learnt from fables to connect the simpler and stronger creatures with the simpler and stronger truths: that a flowing stream cannot befoul its own fountain, and that any one who says it does is a tyrant and a liar; that a mouse is too weak to fight a lion, but too strong for the cords that can hold a lion; that a fox who gets most out of a flat dish may easily get least out of a deep dish; that the crow whom the gods forbid to sing, the gods nevertheless provide with cheese. All these are deep truths deeply graven on the rocks wherever men have passed. It matters nothing how old they are, or how new; they are the alphabet of humanity, which like so many forms of primitive picture-writing employ any living symbol in preference to man. These ancient and universal tales are all of animals; as the latest discoveries in the oldest pre-historic caverns are all of animals. Man, in his simpler states, has always felt that he himself was something too mysterious to be drawn. But the legend he carved under these cruder symbols was everywhere the same.

Whether fables began with Aesop or began with Adam, whether they were German and medieval as Reynard the Fox, or as French and Renaissance as La Fontaine, the upshot is everywhere essentially the same: that superiority is always insolent, because it is always accidental; that pride goes before a fall; and that there is such a thing as being too clever by half. You will not find any other legend but this written upon the rocks by any hand of man. There is every type and time of fable: but there is only one moral to the fable; because there is only one moral to everything.

G. K. **CHESTERTON**

This preface has been lightly edited for clarity.

# Table of Contents



## The Fables

50 :: The Crab and His Mother page 40

# 1 :: The Ant

Ants were once men and made their living by tilling the soil. But, not content with the results of their own work, they were always casting longing eyes upon the crops and fruits of their neighbours, which they stole, whenever they got the chance, and added to their own store. At last their covetousness made Jupiter so angry that he changed them into Ants. But, though their forms were changed, their nature remained the same: and so, to this day, they go about among the cornfields and gather the fruits of others' labour, and store them up for their own use.

***You may punish a thief, but his bent remains.***

Proverbs 2: 15
*Whose ways are crooked,*
*And who are devious in their paths...*

This fable is about an unrepentent condition of the heart:

Jeremiah 17: 9
*The Heart is deceitful above all things*
*And desperately wicked;*
*Who can know it?*

# 2 :: The Apes and The Two Travellers

Two men were travelling together, one of whom never spoke the truth, whereas the other never told a lie: and they came in the course of their travels to the land of Apes. The King of the Apes, hearing of their arrival, ordered them to be brought before him; and by way of impressing them with his magnificence, he received them sitting on a throne, while the Apes, his subjects, were ranged in long rows on either side of him. When the Travellers came into his presence he asked them what they thought of him as a King. The lying Traveller said, "Sire, every one must see that you are a most noble and mighty monarch." "And what do you think of my subjects?" continued the King. "They," said the Traveller, "are in every way worthy of their royal master." The Ape was so delighted with his answer that he gave him a very handsome present. The other Traveller thought that if his companion was rewarded so splendidly for telling a lie, he himself would certainly receive a still greater reward for telling the truth; so, when the Ape turned to him and said, "And what, sir, is your opinion?" he replied, "I think you are a very fine Ape, and all your subjects are fine Apes too." The King of the Apes was so enraged at his reply that he ordered him to be taken away and clawed to death.

Proverbs 25: 11
*A word fitly spoken is like apples of gold in settings of silver.*

# 3 :: The Archer and The Lion

An Archer went up into the hills to get some sport with his bow, and all the animals fled at the sight of him with the exception of the Lion, who stayed behind and challenged him to fight. But he shot an arrow at the Lion and hit him, and said, "There, you see what my messenger can do: just you wait a moment and I'll tackle you myself." The Lion, however, when he felt the sting of the arrow, ran away as fast as his legs could carry him. A fox, who had seen it all happen, said to the Lion, "Come, don't be a coward: why don't you stay and show fight?" But the Lion replied, "You won't get me to stay, not you: why, when he sends a messenger like that before him, he must himself be a terrible fellow to deal with."

***Give a wide berth to those who can do damage at a distance.***

Example: 1 Samuel 18: 11
*And* ***Saul*** *cast the spear, for he said, "I will pin David to the wall!" But David escaped his presence twice.*

## 4 :: The Ass and His Burdens

A Pedlar who owned an **Ass** one day bought a quantity of salt, and loaded up his beast with as much as he could bear. On the way home the Ass stumbled as he was crossing a stream and fell into the water. The salt got thoroughly wetted and much of it melted and drained away, so that, when he got on his legs again, the Ass found his load had become much less heavy. His master, however, drove him back to town and bought more salt, which he added to what remained in the **panniers**, and started out again. No sooner had they reached a stream than the Ass lay down in it, and rose, as before, with a much lighter load. But his master detected the trick, and turning back once more, bought a large number of sponges, and piled them on the back of the Ass. When they came to the stream the Ass again lay down: but this time, as the sponges soaked up large quantities of water, he found, when he got up on his legs, that he had a bigger burden to carry than ever.

***You may play a good card once too often.***

Ecclesiastes 10: 18
*Because of laziness the building decays, And through idleness of hands the house leaks.*

## 5 :: The Ass and His Driver

An **Ass** was being driven down a mountain road, and after jogging along for a while sensibly enough he suddenly quitted the track and rushed to the edge of a precipice. He was just about to leap over the edge when his Driver caught hold of his tail and did his best to pull him back: but pull as he might he couldn't get the Ass to budge from the brink. At last he gave up, crying, "All right, then, get to the bottom your own way; but it's the way to sudden death, as you'll find out quick enough."

# 6 :: The Ass and His Masters

A Gardener had an **Ass** which had a very hard time of it, what with scanty food, heavy loads, and constant beating. The Ass therefore begged **Jupiter** to take him away from the Gardener and hand him over to another master. So Jupiter sent **Mercury** to the Gardener to bid him sell the Ass to a Potter, which he did. But the Ass was as discontented as ever, for he had to work harder than before: so he begged Jupiter for relief a second time, and Jupiter very obligingly arranged that he should be sold to a **Tanner**. But when the Ass saw what his new master's trade was, he cried in despair, "Why wasn't I content to serve either of my former masters, hard as I had to work and badly as I was treated? For they would have buried me decently, but now I shall come in the end to the tanning-vat."

***Servants don't know a good master till they have served a worse.***

Example: Numbers 11: 5
*We remember the fish which we ate freely in Egypt, the cucumbers, the melons, the leeks, the onions, and the garlic...*

1 Timothy 6: 6
***Now godliness with contentment is great gain.***

# 7 :: The Ass and His Purchaser

A Man who wanted to buy an **Ass** went to market, and, coming across a likely-looking beast, arranged with the owner that he should be allowed to take him home on trial to see what he was like. When he reached home, he put him into his stable along with the other asses. The newcomer took a look round, and immediately went and chose a place next to the laziest and greediest beast in the stable. When the master saw this he put a halter on him at once, and led him off and handed him over to his owner again. The latter was a good deal surprised to see him back so soon, and said, "Why, do you mean to say you have tested him already?" "I don't want to put him through any more tests," replied the other: "I could see what sort of beast he is from the companion he chose for himself."

***A man is known by the company he keeps.***

Proverbs 28:7
*Whoso keeps the law is a wise son: but he that is a companion of riotous men shames his father.*

1 Corinthians 15: 33
*Do not be deceived: "Evil company corrupts good habits."*

# 8 :: The Ass and His Shadow

A certain man hired an **Ass** for a journey in summertime, and started out with the owner following behind to drive the beast. By and by, in the heat of the day, they stopped to rest, and the traveller wanted to lie down in the Ass's Shadow; but the owner, who himself wished to be out of the sun, wouldn't let him do that; for he said he had hired the Ass only, and not his Shadow: the other maintained that his bargain secured him complete control of the Ass for the time being. From words they came to blows; and while they were belabouring each other the Ass took to his heels and was soon out of sight.

# 9 :: The Ass and The Dog

An **Ass** and a Dog were on their travels together, and, as they went along, they found a sealed packet lying on the ground. The Ass picked it up, broke the seal, and found it contained some writing, which he proceeded to read out aloud to the Dog. As he read on it turned out to be all about grass and barley and hay—in short, all the kinds of fodder that Asses are fond of. The Dog was a good deal bored with listening to all this, till at last his impatience got the better of him, and he cried, "Just skip a few pages, friend, and see if there isn't something about meat and bones." The Ass glanced all through the packet, but found nothing of the sort, and said so. Then the Dog said in disgust, "Oh, throw it away, do: what's the good of a thing like that?"

# 10 :: The Ass and The Lap-Dog

There was once a man who had an **Ass** and a Lap-dog. The Ass was housed in the stable with plenty of oats and hay to eat and was as well off as an ass could be. The little Dog was made a great pet of by his master, who fondled him and often let him lie in his lap; and if he went out to dinner, he would bring back a tit-bit or two to give him when he ran to meet him on his return. The Ass had, it is true, a good deal of work to do, carting or grinding the corn, or carrying the burdens of the farm: and ere long he became very jealous, contrasting his own life of labour with the ease and idleness of the Lap-dog. At last one day he broke his halter, and frisking into the house just as his master sat down to dinner, he pranced and capered about, mimicking the frolics of the little favourite, upsetting the table and smashing the crockery with his clumsy efforts. Not content with that, he even tried to jump on his master's lap, as he had so often seen the dog allowed to do. At that the servants, seeing the danger their master was in, belaboured the silly Ass with sticks and cudgels, and drove him back to his stable half dead with his beating. "Alas!" he cried, "all this I have brought on myself. Why could I not be satisfied with my natural and honourable position, without wishing to imitate the ridiculous antics of that useless little Lap-dog?"

# 11 :: The Ass and The Mule

A certain man who had an **Ass** and a Mule loaded them both up one day and set out upon a journey. So long as the road was fairly level, the Ass got on very well: but by and by they came to a place among the hills where the road was very rough and steep, and the Ass was at his last gasp. So he begged the Mule to relieve him of a part of his load: but the Mule refused. At last, from sheer weariness, the Ass stumbled and fell down a steep place and was killed. The driver was in despair, but he did the best he could: he added the Ass's load to the Mule's, and he also flayed the Ass and put his skin on the top of the double load. The Mule could only just manage the extra weight, and, as he staggered painfully along, he said to himself, "I have only got what I deserved: if I had been willing to help the Ass at first, I should not now be carrying his load and his skin into the bargain."

# 12 :: The Ass and The Old Peasant

An old Peasant was sitting in a meadow watching his **Ass**, which was grazing close by, when all of a sudden he caught sight of armed men stealthily approaching. He jumped up in a moment, and begged the Ass to fly with him as fast as he could, "Or else," said he, "we shall both be captured by the enemy." But the Ass just looked round lazily and said, "And if so, do you think they'll make me carry heavier loads than I have to now?" "No," said his master. "Oh, well, then," said the Ass, "I don't mind if they do take me, for I shan't be any worse off."

Proverbs 21: 13
*Whoever shuts his ears to the cry of the poor; Will also cry himself and not be heard.*

# 13 :: The Ass and The Wolf

An **Ass** was feeding in a meadow, and, catching sight of his enemy the Wolf in the distance, pretended to be very lame and hobbled painfully along. When the Wolf came up, he asked the Ass how he came to be so lame, and the Ass replied that in going through a hedge he had trodden on a thorn, and he begged the Wolf to pull it out with his teeth, "In case," he said, "when you eat me, it should stick in your throat and hurt you very much." The Wolf said he would, and told the Ass to lift up his foot, and gave his whole mind to getting out the thorn. But the Ass suddenly let out with his heels and fetched the Wolf a fearful kick in the mouth, breaking his teeth; and then he galloped off at full speed. As soon as he could speak the Wolf growled to himself, "It serves me right: my father taught me to kill, and I ought to have stuck to that trade instead of attempting to cure."

Proverbs 3: 13
*Happy is the man who finds wisdom, And the man who gains understanding...*

# 14 :: The Ass Carrying the Image

A certain man put an Image on the back of his **Ass** to take it to one of the temples of the town. As they went along the road all the people they met uncovered and bowed their heads out of reverence for the Image; but the Ass thought they were doing it out of respect for himself, and began to give himself airs accordingly. At last he became so conceited that he imagined he could do as he liked, and, by way of protest against the load he was carrying, he came to a full stop and flatly declined to proceed any further. His driver, finding him so obstinate, hit him hard and long with his stick, saying the while, "Oh, you **dunder-headed** idiot, do you suppose it's come to this, that men pay worship to an Ass?"

***Rude shocks await those who take to themselves the credit that is due to others.***

Isaiah 44: 9
*Those who make an image, all of them are useless, And their precious things shall not profit; They are their own witnesses; They neither see nor know, that they may be ashamed.*

Daniel 5: 20
*But when his heart was lifted up, and his spirit hardened in pride, he was deposed from his kingly throne, and they took his glory from him...*

Proverbs 29: 23
*A man's pride shall bring him low;*
*but the humble in spirit will retain honor.*

# 15 :: The Ass in The Lion's Skin

An **Ass** found a Lion's Skin, and dressed himself up in it. Then he went about frightening every one he met, for they all took him to be a lion, men and beasts alike, and took to their heels when they saw him coming. Elated by the success of his trick, he loudly brayed in triumph. The Fox heard him, and recognised him at once for the Ass he was, and said to him, "Oho, my friend, it's you, is it? I, too, should have been afraid if I hadn't heard your voice."

***Men should be what they seem to be.***

Example: Genesis 20: 2-3
*Now Abraham said of Sarah his wife, "She is my sister." And Abimelech king of Gerar sent and took Sarah. But God came to Abimelech in a dream by night, and said to him, "Indeed you are a dead man because of the woman whom you have taken, for she is a man's wife."*

Mark 12: 14
*And they came up and said to Him, Teacher, we know that You are sincere and what You profess to be, that You cannot lie... (AMP)*

# 16 :: The Ass, The Cock, and The Lion

An **Ass** and a **Cock** were in a cattle-pen together. Presently a Lion, who had been starving for days, came along and was just about to fall upon the Ass and make a meal of him when the Cock, rising to his full height and flapping his wings vigorously, uttered a tremendous crow. Now, if there is one thing that frightens a Lion, it is the crowing of a Cock: and this one had no sooner heard the noise than he fled. The Ass was mightily elated at this, and thought that, if the Lion couldn't face a Cock, he would be still less likely to stand up to an Ass: so he ran out and pursued him. But when the two had got well out of sight and hearing of the Cock, the Lion suddenly turned upon the Ass and ate him up.

***False confidence often leads to disaster.***

Proverbs 28: 26
*He who trusts in his own heart is a fool,*
*But whoever walks wisely will be delivered.*

1 Corinthians 10: 12
*Therefore let him who thinks he stands take heed lest he fall.*

# 17 :: THE ASS, THE FOX, AND THE LION

AN **ASS** AND A FOX WENT INTO PARTNERSHIP and sallied out to forage for food together. They hadn't gone far before they saw a Lion coming their way, at which they were both dreadfully frightened. But the Fox thought he saw a way of saving his own skin, and went boldly up to the Lion and whispered in his ear, "I'll manage that you shall get hold of the Ass without the trouble of stalking him, if you'll promise to let me go free." The Lion agreed to this, and the Fox then rejoined his companion and contrived before long to lead him by a hidden pit, which some hunter had dug as a trap for wild animals, and into which he fell. When the Lion saw that the Ass was safely caught and couldn't get away, it was to the Fox that he first turned his attention, and he soon finished him off, and then at his leisure proceeded to feast upon the Ass.

***Betray a friend, and you'll often find you have ruined yourself.***

Proverbs 1: 18
*But [when these men set a trap for others] they are lying in wait for their own blood; they set an ambush for their own lives. (AMP)*

Proverbs 27: 6
*Faithful are the wounds from a friend, but the kisses of an enemy are deceitful.*

Example: Matthew 27: 3-5
*Then Judas, His betrayer, seeing that He had been condemned, was remorseful and brought back the thirty pieces of silver to the chief priests and elders, saying, "I have sinned by betraying innocent blood." And they said, "What is that to us? You see to it!" Then he threw down the pieces of silver in the temple and departed, and went and hanged himself.*

# 18 :: The Astronomer

There was once an Astronomer whose habit it was to go out at night and observe the stars. One night, as he was walking about outside the town gates, gazing up absorbed into the sky and not looking where he was going, he fell into a dry well. As he lay there groaning, some one passing by heard him, and, coming to the edge of the well, looked down and, on learning what had happened, said, "If you really mean to say that you were looking so hard at the sky that you didn't even see where your feet were carrying you along the ground, it appears to me that you deserve all you've got."

Ecclesiastes 10: 3
*Even when a fool walks along the way, He lacks wisdom, And he shows everyone that he is a fool.*

# 19 :: The Athenian and The Theban

An Athenian and a **Theban** were on the road together, and passed the time in conversation, as is the way of travellers. After discussing a variety of subjects they began to talk about heroes, a topic that tends to be more fertile than edifying. Each of them was lavish in his praises of the heroes of his own city, until eventually the Theban asserted that **Hercules** was the greatest hero who had ever lived on earth, and now occupied a foremost place among the gods; while the Athenian insisted that **Theseus** was far superior, for his fortune had been in every way supremely blessed, whereas Hercules had at one time been forced to act as a servant. And he gained his point, for he was a very glib fellow, like all Athenians; so that the Theban, who was no match for him in talking, cried at last in some disgust, "All right, have your way; I only hope that, when our heroes are angry with us, Athens may suffer from the anger of Hercules, and **Thebes** only from that of Theseus."

# 20 :: The Bald Huntsman

A Man who had lost all his hair took to wearing a wig, and one day he went out hunting. It was blowing rather hard at the time, and he hadn't gone far before a gust of wind caught his hat and carried it off, and his wig too, much to the amusement of the hunt. But he quite entered into the joke, and said, "Ah, well! the hair that wig is made of didn't stick to the head on which it grew; so it's no wonder it won't stick to mine."

# 21 :: The Bald Man and The Fly

A Fly settled on the head of a Bald Man and bit him. In his eagerness to kill it, he hit himself a smart slap. But the Fly escaped, and said to him in derision, "You tried to kill me for just one little bite; what will you do to yourself now, for the heavy smack you have just given yourself?" "Oh, for that blow I bear no grudge," he replied, "for I never intended myself any harm; but as for you, you contemptible insect, who live by sucking human blood, I'd have borne a good deal more than that for the satisfaction of dashing the life out of you!"

# 22 :: The Bat and The Weasels

A Bat fell to the ground and was caught by a Weasel, and was just going to be killed and eaten when it begged to be let go. The Weasel said he couldn't do that because he was an enemy of all birds on principle. "Oh, but," said the Bat, "I'm not a bird at all: I'm a mouse." "So you are," said the Weasel, "now I come to look at you"; and he let it go. Some time after this the Bat was caught in just the same way by another Weasel, and, as before, begged for its life. "No," said the Weasel, "I never let a mouse go by any chance." "But I'm not a mouse," said the Bat; "I'm a bird." "Why, so you are," said the Weasel; and he too let the Bat go.

***Look and see which way the wind blows before you commit yourself.***

Proverbs 14: 15
*The simple believes every word, But the prudent considers well his steps.*

Proverbs 22: 3
*A prudent man foresees evil and hides himself,*
*But the simple pass on and are punished.*

# 23 :: The Bat, The Bramble, and The Seagull

A Bat, a **Bramble**, and a Seagull went into partnership and determined to go on a trading voyage together. The Bat borrowed a sum of money for his venture; the Bramble laid in a stock of clothes of various kinds; and the Seagull took a quantity of lead: and so they set out. By and by a great storm came on, and their boat with all the cargo went to the bottom, but the three travellers managed to reach land. Ever since then the Seagull flies to and fro over the sea, and every now and then dives below the surface, looking for the lead he's lost; while the Bat is so afraid of meeting his creditors that he hides away by day and only comes out at night to feed; and the Bramble catches hold of the clothes of every one who passes by, hoping some day to recognise and recover the lost garments.

> ***All men are more concerned to recover what they lose than to acquire what they lack.***
>
> Luke 15: 8, The Parable of the Lost Coin
> *Or what woman, having ten silver coins, if she loses one coin, does not light a lamp, sweep the house, and search carefully until she finds it?*

# 24 :: The Bear and The Fox

A Bear was once bragging about his generous feelings, and saying how refined he was compared with other animals. There is, in fact, a tradition that a Bear will never touch a dead body. A Fox, who heard him talking in this strain, smiled and said, "My friend, when you are hungry, I only wish you would confine your attention to the dead and leave the living alone."

***A hypocrite deceives no one but himself.***

Psalm 55: 21
*The words of his mouth were smoother than butter,*
*But war was in his heart;*
*His words were softer than oil,*
*Yet they were drawn swords.*

Example: Matthew 23: 27-28
*Woe to you, scribes and Pharisees, hypocrites! For you are like whitewashed tombs which indeed appear beautiful outwardly, but inside are full of dead men's bones and all uncleanness. Even so you also outwardly appear righteous to men, but inside you are full of hypocrisy and lawlessness.*

24 :: THE BEAR AND THE FOX PAGE 20

# 25 :: The Bear and The Travellers

Two Travellers were on the road together, when a Bear suddenly appeared on the scene. Before he observed them, one made for a tree at the side of the road, and climbed up into the branches and hid there. The other was not so nimble as his companion; and, as he could not escape, he threw himself on the ground and pretended to be dead. The Bear came up and sniffed all round him, but he kept perfectly still and held his breath: for they say that a bear will not touch a dead body. The Bear took him for a corpse, and went away. When the coast was clear, the Traveller in the tree came down, and asked the other what it was the Bear had whispered to him when he put his mouth to his ear. The other replied, "He told me never again to travel with a friend who deserts you at the first sign of danger."

***Misfortune tests the sincerity of friendship.***

Proverbs 27: 10
*Do not forsake your own friend or your father's friend,*
*Nor go to your brother's house in the day of your calamity;*
*Better is a neighbor nearby than a brother far away.*

Job 6: 14
*To him who is afflicted, kindness should be shown by his friend,*
*Even though he forsakes the fear of the Almighty.*

Proverbs 17: 17
*A friend loves at all times,*
*And a brother is born for adversity.*

# 26 :: The Bee and Jupiter

A Queen Bee from **Hymettus** flew up to **Olympus** with some fresh honey from the hive as a present to **Jupiter**, who was so pleased with the gift that he promised to give her anything she liked to ask for. She said she would be very grateful if he would give stings to the bees, to kill people who robbed them of their honey. Jupiter was greatly displeased with this request, for he loved mankind: but he had given his word, so he said that stings they should have. The stings he gave them, however, were of such a kind that whenever a bee stings a man the sting is left in the wound and the bee dies.

***Evil wishes, like fowls, come home to roost.***

Proverbs 21: 10
*The soul of the wicked desires evil;*
*His neighbor finds no favor in his eyes.*

Proverbs 26: 27
*Whoever digs a pit will fall into it,*
*And he who rolls a stone will have it roll back on him.*

# 27 :: The Bee-Keeper

A Thief found his way into an **apiary** when the Bee-keeper was away, and stole all the honey. When the Keeper returned and found the hives empty, he was very much upset and stood staring at them for some time. Before long the bees came back from gathering honey, and, finding their hives overturned and the Keeper standing by, they made for him with their stings. At this he fell into a passion and cried, "You ungrateful scoundrels, you let the thief who stole my honey get off scot-free, and then you go and sting me who have always taken such care of you!"

***When you hit back make sure you have got the right man.***

Luke 12: 57
*Yes, and why, even of yourselves, do you not judge what is right?*

# 28 :: The Belly and The Members

The Members of the Body once rebelled against the Belly. "You," they said to the Belly, "live in luxury and sloth, and never do a stroke of work; while we not only have to do all the hard work there is to be done, but are actually your slaves and have to minister to all your wants. Now, we will do so no longer, and you can shift for yourself in the future." They were as good as their word, and left the Belly to starve. The result was just what might have been expected: the whole Body soon began to fail, and the Members and all shared in the general collapse. And then they saw too late how foolish they had been.

I Corinthians 12: 15-18
*If the foot should say, "Because I am not a hand, I am not of the body," is it therefore not of the body? And if the ear should say, "Because I am not an eye, I am not of the body," is it therefore not of the body? If the whole body were an eye, where would be the hearing? If the whole were hearing, where would be the smelling? But now God has set the members, each one of them, in the body just as He pleased.*

# 29 :: The Birds, The Beasts, and The Bat

The Birds were at war with the Beasts, and many battles were fought with varying success on either side. The Bat did not throw in his lot definitely with either party, but when things went well for the Birds he was found fighting in their ranks; when, on the other hand, the Beasts got the upper hand, he was to be found among the Beasts. No one paid any attention to him while the war lasted: but when it was over, and peace was restored, neither the Birds nor the Beasts would have anything to do with so doublefaced a traitor, and so he remains to this day a solitary outcast from both.

# 30 :: The Blackamoor

A Man once bought an **Ethiopian** slave, who had a black skin like all Ethiopians; but his new master thought his colour was due to his late owner's having neglected him, and that all he wanted was a good scrubbing. So he set to work with plenty of soap and hot water, and rubbed away at him with a will, but all to no purpose: his skin remained as black as ever, while the poor wretch all but died from the cold he caught.

# 31 :: The Blacksmith and His Dog

A **Blacksmith** had a little Dog, which used to sleep when his master was at work, but was very wide awake indeed when it was time for meals. One day his master pretended to be disgusted at this, and when he had thrown him a bone as usual, he said, "What on earth is the good of a lazy cur like you? When I am hammering away at my anvil, you just curl up and go to sleep: but no sooner do I stop for a mouthful of food than you wake up and wag your tail to be fed."

***Those who will not work deserve to starve.***

Proverbs 6: 6
*Go to the ant, you sluggard;*
*consider her ways and be wise!*

Proverbs 13: 4
*The soul of a lazy man desires, and has nothing;*
*But the soul of the diligent shall be made rich.*

2 Thessalonians 3: 10
*For even when we were with you, we commanded you this: If anyone will not work, neither shall he eat.*

# 32 :: The Blind Man and The Cub

There was once a Blind Man who had so fine a sense of touch that, when any animal was put into his hands, he could tell what it was merely by the feel of it. One day the Cub of a Wolf was put into his hands, and he was asked what it was. He felt it for some time, and then said, "Indeed, I am not sure whether it is a Wolf's Cub or a Fox's: but this I know—it would never do to trust it in a sheepfold."

***Evil tendencies are early shown.***

Proverbs 20: 11
*Even a child is known by his deeds,*
*Whether what he does is pure and right.*

# 33 :: The Boasting Traveller

A Man once went abroad on his travels, and when he came home he had wonderful tales to tell of the things he had done in foreign countries. Among other things, he said he had taken part in a jumping-match at **Rhodes**, and had done a wonderful jump which no one could beat. "Just go to Rhodes and ask them," he said; "every one will tell you it's true." But one of those who were listening said, "If you can jump as well as all that, we needn't go to Rhodes to prove it. Let's just imagine this is Rhodes for a minute: and now—jump!"

***Deeds, not words.***

Proverbs 20: 11
*Even a child is known by his deeds, whether what he does is pure and right.*

1 John 3: 18
*My little children, let us not love in word or in tongue, but in deed and in truth.*

# 34 :: The Boy and The Filberts

A Boy put his hand into a jar of **Filberts**, and grasped as many as his fist could possibly hold. But when he tried to pull it out again, he found he couldn't do so, for the neck of the jar was too small to allow of the passage of so large a handful. Unwilling to lose his nuts but unable to withdraw his hand, he burst into tears. A bystander, who saw where the trouble lay, said to him, "Come, my boy, don't be so greedy: be content with half the amount, and you'll be able to get your hand out without difficulty."

***Do not attempt too much at once.***

Proverbs 23: 4
*Do not overwork to be rich;*
*Because of your own understanding, cease!*

# 35 :: The Boy and The Nettles

A Boy was gathering berries from a hedge when his hand was stung by a **Nettle**. Smarting with the pain, he ran to tell his mother, and said to her between his sobs, "I only touched it ever so lightly, Mother." "That's just why you got stung, my son," she said; "if you had grasped it firmly, it wouldn't have hurt you in the least."

# 36 :: The Boy and The Snails

A Farmer's Boy went looking for Snails, and, when he had picked up both his hands full, he set about making a fire at which to roast them; for he meant to eat them. When it got well alight and the Snails began to feel the heat, they gradually withdrew more and more into their shells with the hissing noise they always make when they do so. When the Boy heard it, he said, "You abandoned creatures, how can you find heart to whistle when your houses are burning?"

# 37 :: The Boy Bathing

A Boy was bathing in a river and got out of his depth, and was in great danger of being drowned. A man who was passing along a road heard his cries for help, and went to the riverside and began to scold him for being so careless as to get into deep water, but made no attempt to help him. "Oh, sir," cried the Boy, "please help me first and scold me afterwards."

***Give assistance, not advice, in a crisis.***

Job 38: 2
*Who is this who darkens counsel,*
*By words without knowledge?*

Example: Luke 10: 33-34
*But a certain Samaritan, as he journeyed, came where he was. And when he saw him, he had compassion. So he went to him and bandaged his wounds, pouring on oil and wine; and he set him on his own animal, brought him to an inn, and took care of him.*

# 38 :: The Boys and The Frogs

Some mischievous Boys were playing on the edge of a pond, and, catching sight of some Frogs swimming about in the shallow water, they began to amuse themselves by pelting them with stones, and they killed several of them. At last one of the Frogs put his head out of the water and said, "Oh, stop! stop! I beg of you: what is sport to you is death to us."

Hosea 6: 6
*For I desire mercy and not sacrifice, And the knowledge of God more than burnt offerings.*

I Peter 3: 8
*Finally, all of you be of one mind, having compassion for one another; love as brothers, be tenderhearted, be courteous.*

# 39 :: The Bull and The Calf

A full-grown Bull was struggling to force his huge bulk through the narrow entrance to a cow-house where his stall was, when a young Calf came up and said to him, "If you'll step aside a moment, I'll show you the way to get through." The Bull turned upon him an amused look. "I knew that way," said he, "before you were born."

# 40 :: The Butcher and His Customers

Two Men were buying meat at a Butcher's stall in the market-place, and, while the Butcher's back was turned for a moment, one of them snatched up a joint and hastily thrust it under the other's cloak, where it could not be seen. When the Butcher turned round, he missed the meat at once, and charged them with having stolen it: but the one who had taken it said he hadn't got it, and the one who had got it said he hadn't taken it. The Butcher felt sure they were deceiving him, but he only said, "You may cheat me with your lying, but you can't cheat the gods, and they won't let you off so lightly."

***Prevarication often amounts to perjury.***

Proverbs 4: 24
*Put away from you false and dishonest speech,*
*and willful and contrary talk put far from you. (AMP)*

An alternate meaning of the fable stems from the words of the Butcher, "You may cheat me with your lying, but you can't cheat the gods, and they won't let you off so lightly." In Scripture we see that the reward for evil or good deeds ultimately comes.

Matthew 13: 30
*Let both grow together until the harvest, and at the time of harvest I will say to the reapers, "First gather together the tares and bind them in bundles to burn them, but gather the wheat into my barn."*

Psalm 37: 7-9
*Rest in the Lord, and wait patiently for Him; Do not fret because of him who prospers in his way, Because of the man who brings wicked schemes to pass. Cease from anger, and forsake wrath; Do not fret—it only causes harm. For evildoers shall be cut off; But those who wait on the Lord, They shall inherit the earth.*

# 41 :: The Cage-Bird and The Bat

A Singing-bird was confined in a cage which hung outside a window, and had a way of singing at night when all other birds were asleep. One night a Bat came and clung to the bars of the cage, and asked the Bird why she was silent by day and sang only at night. "I have a very good reason for doing so," said the Bird: "it was once when I was singing in the daytime that a **fowler** was attracted by my voice, and set his nets for me and caught me. Since then I have never sung except by night." But the Bat replied, "It is no use your doing that now when you are a prisoner: if only you had done so before you were caught, you might still have been free."

***Precautions are useless after the event.***

Example: Matthew 25: 8-10
*And the foolish said to the wise, 'Give us some of your oil, for our lamps are going out.' But the wise answered, saying, 'No, lest there should not be enough for us and you; but go rather to those who sell, and buy for yourselves.' And while they went to buy, the bridegroom came, and those who were ready went in with him to the wedding; and the door was shut.*

# 42 :: The Cat and The Birds

A Cat heard that the Birds in an aviary were ailing. So he got himself up as a doctor, and, taking with him a set of the instruments proper to his profession, presented himself at the door, and inquired after the health of the Birds. "We shall do very well," they replied, without letting him in, "when we've seen the last of you."

***A villain may disguise himself, but he will not deceive the wise.***

Matthew 7: 15
*Beware of false prophets, who come to you in sheep's clothing, but inwardly they are ravenous wolves*

# 43 :: The Cat and The Cock

A Cat pounced on a **Cock**, and cast about for some good excuse for making a meal off him, for Cats don't as a rule eat Cocks, and she knew she ought not to. At last she said, "You make a great nuisance of yourself at night by crowing and keeping people awake: so I am going to make an end of you." But the Cock defended himself by saying that he crowed in order that men might wake up and set about the day's work in good time, and that they really couldn't very well do without him. "That may be," said the Cat, "but whether they can or not, I'm not going without my dinner"; and she killed and ate him.

***The want of a good excuse never kept a villain from crime.***

Example Genesis 4: 9
*Then the Lord said to Cain, "Where is Abel your brother?" He said, "I do not know. Am I my brother's keeper?"*

Example: Matthew 25: 24
*Then he who had received the one talent came and said, 'Lord, I knew you to be a hard man, reaping where you have not sown, and gathering where you have not scattered seed.'*

# 44 :: The Cat and The Mice

There was once a house that was overrun with Mice. A Cat heard of this, and said to herself, "That's the place for me," and off she went and took up her quarters in the house, and caught the Mice one by one and ate them. At last the Mice could stand it no longer, and they determined to take to their holes and stay there. "That's awkward," said the Cat to herself: "the only thing to do is to coax them out by a trick." So she considered a while, and then climbed up the wall and let herself hang down by her hind legs from a peg, and pretended to be dead. By and by a Mouse peeped out and saw the Cat hanging there. "Aha!" it cried, "you're very clever, madam, no doubt: but you may turn yourself into a bag of meal hanging there, if you like, yet you won't catch us coming anywhere near you."

***If you are wise you won't be deceived by the innocent airs of those whom you have once found to be dangerous.***

Example: Jeremiah 9: 5
*Everyone will deceive his neighbor, And will not speak the truth; They have taught their tongue to speak lies; They weary themselves to commit iniquity.*

James 3: 11
*Does a spring send forth fresh water and bitter from the same opening?*

# 45 :: The Charcoal-Burner and The Fuller

There was once a **Charcoal-burner** who lived and worked by himself. A **Fuller**, however, happened to come and settle in the same neighbourhood; and the Charcoal-burner, having made his acquaintance and finding he was an agreeable sort of fellow, asked him if he would come and share his house: "We shall get to know one another better that way," he said, "and, beside, our household expenses will be diminished." The Fuller thanked him, but replied, "I couldn't think of it, sir: why, everything I take such pains to whiten would be blackened in no time by your charcoal."

# 46 :: The Charger and The Miller

A Horse, who had been used to carry his rider into battle, felt himself growing old and chose to work in a mill instead. He now no longer found himself stepping out proudly to the beating of the drums, but was compelled to slave away all day grinding the corn. Bewailing his hard lot, he said one day to the **Miller**, "Ah me! I was once a splendid war-horse, gaily caparisoned, and attended by a **groom** whose sole duty was to see to my wants. How different is my present condition! I wish I had never given up the battlefield for the mill." The Miller replied with asperity, "It's no use your regretting the past. Fortune has many ups and downs: you must just take them as they come."

# 47 :: The Clown and The Countryman

A Nobleman announced his intention of giving a public entertainment in the theatre, and offered splendid prizes to all who had any novelty to exhibit at the performance. The announcement attracted a crowd of conjurers, jugglers, and acrobats, and among the rest a Clown, very popular with the crowd, who let it be known that he was going to give an entirely new turn. When the day of the performance came, the theatre was filled from top to bottom some time before the entertainment began. Several performers exhibited their tricks, and then the popular favourite came on empty-handed and alone. At once there was a hush of expectation: and he, letting his head fall upon his breast, imitated the squeak of a pig to such perfection that the audience insisted on his producing the animal, which, they said, he must have somewhere concealed about his person. He, however, convinced them that there was no pig there, and then the applause was deafening. Among the spectators was a Countryman, who disparaged the Clown's performance and announced that he would give a much superior exhibition of the same trick on the following day. Again the theatre was filled to overflowing, and again the Clown gave his imitation amidst the cheers of the crowd. The Countryman, meanwhile, before going on the stage, had secreted a young porker under his smock; and when the spectators derisively bade him do better if he could, he gave it a pinch in the ear and made it squeal loudly. But they all with one voice shouted out that the Clown's imitation was much more true to life. Thereupon he produced the pig from under his smock and said sarcastically, "There, that shows what sort of judges you are!"

# 48 :: The Cobbler Turned Doctor

A very unskilful **Cobbler**, finding himself unable to make a living at his trade, gave up mending boots and took to doctoring instead. He gave out that he had the secret of a universal antidote against all poisons, and acquired no small reputation, thanks to his talent for puffing himself. One day, however, he fell very ill; and the King of the country bethought him that he would test the value of his remedy. Calling, therefore, for a cup, he poured out a dose of the antidote, and, under pretence of mixing poison with it, added a little water, and commanded him to drink it. Terrified by the fear of being poisoned, the Cobbler confessed that he knew nothing about medicine, and that his antidote was worthless. Then the King summoned his subjects and addressed them as follows: "What folly could be greater than yours? Here is this Cobbler to whom no one will send his boots to be mended, and yet you have not hesitated to entrust him with your lives!"

Jeremiah 17: 9
*The heart is deceitful above all things,*
*And desperately wicked;*
*Who can know it?*

Example of disguise for unjust ends can be found in the story of Jacob and Esau in Genesis 27.

Genesis 27: 18-19
*So he went to his father and said, "My father."*
*And he said, "Here I am. Who are you, my son?"*
*Jacob said to his father, "I am Esau your firstborn; I have done just as you told me; please arise, sit and eat of my game, that your soul may bless me."*

# 49 :: The Cock and The Jewel

A **Cock**, scratching the ground for something to eat, turned up a Jewel that had by chance been dropped there. "Ho!" said he, "a fine thing you are, no doubt, and, had your owner found you, great would his joy have been. But for me! give me a single grain of corn before all the jewels in the world."

# 50 :: The Crab and His Mother

An Old Crab said to her son, "Why do you walk sideways like that, my son? You ought to walk straight." The Young Crab replied, "Show me how, dear mother, and I'll follow your example." The Old Crab tried, but tried in vain, and then saw how foolish she had been to find fault with her child.

***Example is better than precept.***

John 13: 15
*For I have given you an example that you should do as I have done to you.*

# 51 :: The Crab and The Fox

A Crab once left the sea-shore and went and settled in a meadow some way inland, which looked very nice and green and seemed likely to be a good place to feed in. But a hungry Fox came along and spied the Crab and caught him. Just as he was going to be eaten up, the Crab said, "This is just what I deserve; for I had no business to leave my natural home by the sea and settle here as though I belonged to the land."

***Be content with your lot.***

Philippians 4: 11
*...for I have learned in whatever state I am, to be content.*

Luke 12: 29
*And do not seek what you should eat or what you should drink, nor have an anxious mind.*

# 52 :: The Crow and The Pitcher

A thirsty Crow found a Pitcher with some water in it, but so little was there that, try as she might, she could not reach it with her beak, and it seemed as though she would die of thirst within sight of the remedy. At last she hit upon a clever plan. She began dropping pebbles into the Pitcher, and with each pebble the water rose a little higher until at last it reached the brim, and the knowing bird was enabled to quench her thirst.

***Necessity is the mother of invention.***

Example: Judges 7: 16
*Then he [Gideon] divided the three hundred men into three companies, and he put a trumpet into every man's hand, with empty pitchers, and torches inside the pitchers.*

To read the entire story of Gideon's clever defeat of the Midianites, see Judges 6-8.

Proverbs 16: 1
*The plans of the mind and orderly thinking belong to man,*
*But from the Lord comes the [wise] answer of the tongue. (AMP)*

# 53 :: The Crow and The Raven

A Crow became very jealous of a Raven, because the latter was regarded by men as a bird of omen which foretold the future, and was accordingly held in great respect by them. She was very anxious to get the same sort of reputation herself; and, one day, seeing some travellers approaching, she flew on to a branch of a tree at the roadside and cawed as loud as she could. The travellers were in some dismay at the sound, for they feared it might be a bad omen; till one of them, spying the Crow, said to his companions, "It's all right, my friends, we can go on without fear, for it's only a crow and that means nothing."

***Those who pretend to be something they are not only make themselves ridiculous.***

Job 20: 5
*That the triumphing of the wicked is short,*
*And the joy of the hypocrite is but for a moment?*

Example: Luke 18: 11
*The Pharisee stood and prayed thus with himself, 'God, I thank You that I am not like other men—extortioners, unjust, adulterers, or even as this tax collector.'*

# 54 :: The Crow and The Snake

A hungry Crow spied a Snake lying asleep in a sunny spot, and, picking it up in his claws, he was carrying it off to a place where he could make a meal of it without being disturbed, when the Snake reared its head and bit him. It was a poisonous Snake, and the bite was fatal, and the dying Crow said, "What a cruel fate is mine! I thought I had made a lucky find, and it has cost me my life!"

# 55 :: The Crow and The Swan

A Crow was filled with envy on seeing the beautiful white plumage of a Swan, and thought it was due to the water in which the Swan constantly bathed and swam. So he left the neighbourhood of the altars, where he got his living by picking up bits of the meat offered in sacrifice, and went and lived among the pools and streams. But though he bathed and washed his feathers many times a day, he didn't make them any whiter, and at last died of hunger into the bargain.

***You may change your habits, but not your nature.***

Proverbs 22: 6
*Train up a child in the way he should go,*
*And when he is old he will not depart from it.*

# 56 :: The Debtor and His Sow

A Man of Athens fell into debt and was pressed for the money by his creditor; but he had no means of paying at the time, so he begged for delay. But the creditor refused and said he must pay at once. Then the Debtor fetched a **Sow**—the only one he had—and took her to market to offer her for sale. It happened that his creditor was there too. Presently a buyer came along and asked if the Sow produced good litters. "Yes," said the Debtor, "very fine ones; and the remarkable thing is that she produces females at the Mysteries and males at the **Panathenea**." (Festivals these were: and the Athenians always sacrifice a sow at one, and a **boar** at the other; while at the **Dionysia** they sacrifice a kid.) At that the creditor, who was standing by, put in, "Don't be surprised, sir; why, still better, at the Dionysia this Sow has kids!"

## 57 :: The Dog and The Cook

A rich man once invited a number of his friends and acquaintances to a banquet. His dog thought it would be a good opportunity to invite another Dog, a friend of his; so he went to him and said, "My master is giving a feast: there'll be a fine spread, so come and dine with me to-night." The Dog thus invited came, and when he saw the preparations being made in the kitchen he said to himself, "My word, I'm in luck: I'll take care to eat enough to-night to last me two or three days." At the same time he wagged his tail briskly, by way of showing his friend how delighted he was to have been asked. But just then the Cook caught sight of him, and, in his annoyance at seeing a strange Dog in the kitchen, caught him up by the hind legs and threw him out of the window. He had a nasty fall, and limped away as quickly as he could, howling dismally. Presently some other dogs met him, and said, "Well, what sort of a dinner did you get?" To which he replied, "I had a splendid time: the wine was so good, and I drank so much of it, that I really don't remember how I got out of the house!"

***Be shy of favours bestowed at the expense of others.***

Proverbs 23: 6
*Do not eat the bread of a miser, nor desire his delicacies.*

# 58 :: The Dog and The Shadow

A Dog was crossing a plank bridge over a stream with a piece of meat in his mouth, when he happened to see his own reflection in the water. He thought it was another dog with a piece of meat twice as big; so he let go his own, and flew at the other dog to get the larger piece. But, of course, all that happened was that he got neither; for one was only a shadow, and the other was carried away by the current.

# 59 :: The Dog and The Sow

A Dog and a Sow were arguing and each claimed that its own young ones were finer than those of any other animal. "Well," said the **Sow** at last, "mine can see, at any rate, when they come into the world: but yours are born blind."

# 60 :: The Dog and The Wolf

A Dog was lying in the sun before a farmyard gate when a Wolf pounced upon him and was just going to eat him up; but he begged for his life and said, "You see how thin I am and what a wretched meal I should make you now: but if you will only wait a few days my master is going to give a feast. All the rich scraps and pickings will fall to me and I shall get nice and fat: then will be the time for you to eat me." The Wolf thought this was a very good plan and went away. Some time afterwards he came to the farmyard again, and found the Dog lying out of reach on the stable roof. "Come down," he called, "and be eaten: you remember our agreement?" But the Dog said coolly, "My friend, if ever you catch me lying down by the gate there again, don't you wait for any feast."

***Once bitten, twice shy.***

Proverbs 4: 13
*Take firm hold of instruction, do not let go; Keep her, for she is your life.*

Proverbs 10: 17
*He who keeps instruction is in the way of life, But he who refuses correction goes astray.*

# 61 :: The Dog Chasing A Wolf

A Dog was chasing a Wolf, and as he ran he thought what a fine fellow he was, and what strong legs he had, and how quickly they covered the ground. "Now, there's this Wolf," he said to himself, "what a poor creature he is: he's no match for me, and he knows it and so he runs away." But the Wolf looked round just then and said, "Don't you imagine I'm running away from you, my friend: it's your master I'm afraid of."

# 62 :: The Dog In The Manger

A Dog was lying in a Manger on the hay which had been put there for the cattle, and when they came and tried to eat, he growled and snapped at them and wouldn't let them get at their food. "What a selfish beast," said one of them to his companions; "he can't eat himself and yet he won't let those eat who can."

# 63 :: The Dog, The Cock, and The Fox

A Dog and a **Cock** became great friends, and agreed to travel together. At nightfall the Cock flew up into the branches of a tree to roost, while the Dog curled himself up inside the trunk, which was hollow. At break of day the Cock woke up and crew, as usual. A Fox heard, and, wishing to make a breakfast of him, came and stood under the tree and begged him to come down. "I should so like," said he, "to make the acquaintance of one who has such a beautiful voice." The Cock replied, "Would you just wake my porter who sleeps at the foot of the tree? He'll open the door and let you in." The Fox accordingly rapped on the trunk, when out rushed the Dog and tore him in pieces.

# 64 :: The Dogs and The Fox

Some Dogs once found a lion's skin, and were worrying it with their teeth. Just then a Fox came by, and said, "You think yourselves very brave, no doubt; but if that were a live lion you'd find his claws a good deal sharper than your teeth."

# 65 :: The Dogs and The Hides

Once upon a time a number of Dogs, who were famished with hunger, saw some Hides steeping in a river, but couldn't get at them because the water was too deep. So they put their heads together, and decided to drink away at the river till it was shallow enough for them to reach the Hides. But long before that happened they burst themselves with drinking.

## 66 :: The Dolphins, The Whale, and The Sprat

The Dolphins quarrelled with the Whales, and before very long they began fighting with one another. The battle was very fierce, and had lasted some time without any sign of coming to an end, when a **Sprat** thought that perhaps he could stop it; so he stepped in and tried to persuade them to give up fighting and make friends. But one of the Dolphins said to him contemptuously, "We would rather go on fighting till we're all killed than be reconciled by a Sprat like you!"

## 67 :: The Eagle and His Captor

A Man once caught an Eagle, and after clipping his wings turned him loose among the fowls in his hen-house, where he moped in a corner, looking very dejected and forlorn. After a while his Captor was glad enough to sell him to a neighbour, who took him home and let his wings grow again. As soon as he had recovered the use of them, the Eagle flew out and caught a **hare**, which he brought home and presented to his benefactor. A fox observed this, and said to the Eagle, "Don't waste your gifts on him! Go and give them to the man who first caught you; make him your friend, and then perhaps he won't catch you and clip your wings a second time."

## 68 :: The Eagle and The Arrow

An Eagle sat perched on a lofty rock, keeping a sharp look-out for prey. A huntsman, concealed in a cleft of the mountain and on the watch for game, spied him there and shot an Arrow at him. The shaft struck him full in the breast and pierced him through and through. As he lay in the agonies of death, he turned his eyes upon the Arrow. "Ah! cruel fate!" he cried, "that I should perish thus: but oh! fate more cruel still, that the Arrow which kills me should be winged with an Eagle's feathers!"

# 69 :: The Eagle and The Beetle

An Eagle was chasing a **hare**, which was running for dear life and was at her wits' end to know where to turn for help. Presently she espied a Beetle, and begged it to aid her. So when the Eagle came up the Beetle warned her not to touch the **Hare**, which was under its protection. But the Eagle never noticed the Beetle because it was so small, seized the Hare and ate her up. The Beetle never forgot this, and used to keep an eye on the Eagle's nest, and whenever the Eagle laid an egg it climbed up and rolled it out of the nest and broke it. At last the Eagle got so worried over the loss of her eggs that she went up to **Jupiter**, who is the special protector of Eagles, and begged him to give her a safe place to nest in: so he let her lay her eggs in his lap. But the Beetle noticed this and made a ball of dirt the size of an Eagle's egg, and flew up and deposited it in Jupiter's lap. When Jupiter saw the dirt, he stood up to shake it out of his robe, and, forgetting about the eggs, he shook them out too, and they were broken just as before. Ever since then, they say, Eagles never lay their eggs at the season when Beetles are about.

***The weak will sometimes find ways to avenge an insult, even upon the strong.***

Romans 12: 19
*Beloved, do not avenge yourselves, but rather give place to wrath; for it is written, "Vengeance is Mine, I will repay," says the Lord.*

Romans 12: 9
*Let love be without hypocrisy. Abhor what is evil. Cling to what is good.*

# 70 :: The Eagle and The Cocks

There were two Cocks in the same farmyard, and they fought to decide who should be master. When the fight was over, the beaten one went and hid himself in a dark corner; while the victor flew up on to the roof of the stables and crowed lustily. But an Eagle espied him from high up in the sky, and swooped down and carried him off. Forthwith the other **Cock** came out of his corner and ruled the roost without a rival.

***Pride comes before a fall.***

Example: 2 Chronicles 32: 26
*Then Hezekiah humbled himself for the pride of his heart, he and the inhabitants of Jerusalem, so that the wrath of the Lord did not come upon them in the days of Hezekiah.*

Proverbs 16: 18
*Pride goes before destruction,*
*And a haughty spirit before a fall.*

Proverbs 13: 10
*By pride comes nothing but strife,*
*But with the well-advised is wisdom.*

# 71 :: The Eagle and The Fox

An Eagle and a Fox became great friends and determined to live near one another: they thought that the more they saw of each other the better friends they would be. So the Eagle built a nest at the top of a high tree, while the Fox settled in a thicket at the foot of it and produced a litter of cubs. One day the Fox went out foraging for food, and the Eagle, who also wanted food for her young, flew down into the thicket, caught up the Fox's cubs, and carried them up into the tree for a meal for herself and her family. When the Fox came back, and found out what had happened, she was not so much sorry for the loss of her cubs as furious because she couldn't get at the Eagle and pay her out for her treachery. So she sat down not far off and cursed her. But it wasn't long before she had her revenge. Some villagers happened to be sacrificing a goat on a neighbouring altar, and the Eagle flew down and carried off a piece of burning flesh to her nest. There was a strong wind blowing, and the nest caught fire, with the result that her fledglings fell half-roasted to the ground. Then the Fox ran to the spot and devoured them in full sight of the Eagle.

***False faith may escape human punishment, but cannot escape the divine.***

Ecclesiastes 12: 14
*For God will bring every work into judgment,*
*Including every secret thing, Whether good or evil.*

Luke 8: 17
*For nothing is secret that will not be revealed, nor anything hidden that will not be known and come to light.*

# 72 :: The Eagle, The Cat, and The Wild Sow

An Eagle built her nest at the top of a high tree; a Cat with her family occupied a hollow in the trunk half-way down; and a Wild **Sow** and her young took up their quarters at the foot. They might have got on very well as neighbours had it not been for the evil cunning of the Cat. Climbing up to the Eagle's nest she said to the Eagle, "You and I are in the greatest possible danger. That dreadful creature, the Sow, who is always to be seen grubbing away at the foot of the tree, means to uproot it, that she may devour your family and mine at her ease." Having thus driven the Eagle almost out of her senses with terror, the Cat climbed down the tree, and said to the Sow, "I must warn you against that dreadful bird, the Eagle. She is only waiting her chance to fly down and carry off one of your little pigs when you take them out, to feed her brood with." She succeeded in frightening the Sow as much as the Eagle. Then she returned to her hole in the trunk, from which, feigning to be afraid, she never came forth by day. Only by night did she creep out unseen to procure food for her kittens. The Eagle, meanwhile was afraid to stir from her nest, and the Sow dared not leave her home among the roots: so that in time both they and their families perished of hunger, and their dead bodies supplied the Cat with ample food for her growing family.

Isaiah 32: 7
*Also the schemes of the schemer are evil; He devises wicked plans To destroy the poor with lying words...*

Galatians 5: 15
*But if you bite and devour one another, beware lest you be consumed by one another!*

# 73 :: The Eagle, The Jackdaw, and The Shepherd

One day a **Jackdaw** saw an Eagle swoop down on a lamb and carry it off in its talons. "My word," said the Jackdaw, "I'll do that myself." So it flew high up into the air, and then came shooting down with a great whirring of wings on to the back of a big ram. It had no sooner alighted than its claws got caught fast in the wool, and nothing it could do was of any use: there it stuck, flapping away, and only making things worse instead of better. By and by up came the Shepherd. "Oho," he said, "so that's what you'd be doing, is it?" And he took the Jackdaw, and clipped its wings and carried it home to his children. It looked so odd that they didn't know what to make of it. "What sort of bird is it, father?" they asked. "It's a Jackdaw," he replied, "and nothing but a Jackdaw: but it wants to be taken for an Eagle."

***If you attempt what is beyond your power, your trouble will be wasted and you court not only misfortune but ridicule.***

Proverbs 1: 4
*To give prudence to the simple,*
*To the young man knowledge and discretion.*

Luke 14: 28
*For which of you, intending to build a tower, does not sit down first and count the cost, whether he has enough to finish it.*

# 74 :: The Escaped Jackdaw

A Man caught a **Jackdaw** and tied a piece of string to one of its legs, and then gave it to his children for a pet. But the Jackdaw didn't at all like having to live with people; so, after a while, when he seemed to have become fairly tame and they didn't watch him so closely, he slipped away and flew back to his old haunts. Unfortunately, the string was still on his leg, and before long it got entangled in the branches of a tree and the Jackdaw couldn't get free, try as he would. He saw it was all up with him, and cried in despair, "Alas, in gaining my freedom I have lost my life."

# 75 :: The Farmer and Fortune

A Farmer was ploughing one day on his farm when he turned up a pot of golden coins with his plough. He was overjoyed at his discovery, and from that time forth made an offering daily at the shrine of the **Goddess of the Earth**. **Fortune** was displeased at this, and came to him and said, "My man, why do you give Earth the credit for the gift which I bestowed upon you? You never thought of thanking me for your good luck; but should you be unlucky enough to lose what you have gained I know very well that I, Fortune, should then come in for all the blame."

***Show gratitude where gratitude is due.***

God asks us repeatedly in Scripture to be thankful for His many gifts to men. There are so many Scriptures on thankfulness that we include only a few for meditation.

Psalm 107: 31
*Oh that men would give thanks to the Lord for His goodness,*
*And for His wonderful works to the children of men!*

1 Thessalonians 5: 18
*In everything give thanks; for this is the will of God in Christ Jesus for you.*

# 76 :: THE FARMER AND HIS DOGS

A FARMER WAS SNOWED UP IN HIS FARMSTEAD BY A SEVERE STORM, and was unable to go out and procure provisions for himself and his family. So he first killed his sheep and used them for food; then, as the storm still continued, he killed his goats; and, last of all, as the weather showed no signs of improving, he was compelled to kill his oxen and eat them. When his Dogs saw the various animals being killed and eaten in turn, they said to one another, "We had better get out of this or we shall be the next to go!"

# 77 :: THE FARMER AND HIS SONS

A FARMER, BEING AT DEATH'S DOOR, and desiring to impart to his Sons a secret of much moment, called them round him and said, "My sons, I am shortly about to die; I would have you know, therefore, that in my vineyard there lies a hidden treasure. Dig, and you will find it." As soon as their father was dead, the Sons took spade and fork and turned up the soil of the vineyard over and over again, in their search for the treasure which they supposed to lie buried there. They found none, however: but the vines, after so thorough a digging, produced a crop such as had never before been seen.

Genesis 26: 12
*Then Isaac sowed in that land, and reaped in the same year a hundredfold; and the Lord blessed him.*

Galatians 6: 7
*Do not be deceived, God is not mocked; for whatever a man sows, that he will also reap.*

# 78 :: The Farmer and The Fox

A Farmer was greatly annoyed by a Fox, which came prowling about his yard at night and carried off his fowls. So he set a trap for him and caught him; and in order to be revenged upon him, he tied a bunch of **tow** to his tail and set fire to it and let him go. As ill-luck would have it, however, the Fox made straight for the fields where the corn was standing ripe and ready for cutting. It quickly caught fire and was all burnt up, and the Farmer lost all his harvest.

***Revenge is a two-edged sword.***

Example: Judges 15: 4-5
*And Samson said to them, "This time I shall be blameless regarding the Philistines if I harm them!" Then Samson went and caught three hundred foxes; and he took torches, turned the foxes tail to tail, and put a torch between each pair of tails. When he had set the torches on fire, he let the foxes go into the standing grain of the Philistines, and burned up the shocks and the standing grain, as well as the vineyards and olive groves.*

Matthew 5: 25
*Agree with your adversary quickly, while you are on the way with him, lest your adversary deliver you to the judge, the judge hand you over to the officer and you be thrown into prison.*

Because revenge harms the doer *and* the receiver we are enjoined to let God, who judges correctly, repay wrongs.

Romans 12: 19
*Beloved, do not avenge yourselves, but rather give place to wrath; for it is written, "Vengeance is Mine, I will repay," says the Lord.*

(Also, Deuteronomy 32: 35)

# 79 :: The Farmer and The Stork

A Farmer set some traps in a field which he had lately sown with corn, in order to catch the cranes which came to pick up the seed. When he returned to look at his traps he found several cranes caught, and among them a **Stork**, which begged to be let go, and said, "You ought not to kill me: I am not a **crane**, but a Stork, as you can easily see by my feathers, and I am the most honest and harmless of birds." But the Farmer replied, "It's nothing to me what you are: I find you among these cranes, who ruin my crops, and, like them, you shall suffer."

***If you choose bad companions no one will believe that you are anything but bad yourself.***

A more common form of the moral for this fable is
***Birds of a feather flock together.***

Proverbs 28: 7
*Whoever keeps the law is a discerning son,*
*But a companion of gluttons shames his father.*

1 Corinthians 15: 33
*Do not be deceived: "Evil company corrupts good habits."*

# 80 :: The Farmer and The Viper

One winter a Farmer found a **Viper** frozen and numb with cold, and out of pity picked it up and placed it in his bosom. The Viper was no sooner revived by the warmth than it turned upon its benefactor and inflicted a fatal bite upon him; and as the poor man lay dying, he cried, "I have only got what I deserved, for taking compassion on so villainous a creature."

***Kindness is thrown away upon the evil.***

Psalm 52: 3
*You love evil more than good,*
*Lying rather than speaking righteousness. Selah.*

# 81 :: The Farmer, His Boy, and The Rooks

A Farmer had just sown a field of wheat, and was keeping a careful watch over it, for numbers of **Rooks** and **Starlings** kept continually settling on it and eating up the grain. Along with him went his Boy, carrying a sling: and whenever the Farmer asked for the sling the starlings understood what he said and warned the Rooks and they were off in a moment. So the Farmer hit on a trick. "My lad," said he, "we must get the better of these birds somehow. After this, when I want the sling, I won't say 'sling,' but just 'humph!' and you must then hand me the sling quickly." Presently back came the whole flock. "Humph!" said the Farmer; but the Starlings took no notice, and he had time to sling several stones among them, hitting one on the head, another in the legs, and another in the wing, before they got out of range. As they made all haste away they met some Cranes, who asked them what the matter was. "Matter?" said one of the Rooks; "it's those rascals, men, that are the matter. Don't you go near them. They have a way of saying one thing and meaning another which has just been the death of several of our poor friends."

# 82 :: The Father and His Daughters

A Man had two Daughters, one of whom he gave in marriage to a gardener, and the other to a potter. After a time he thought he would go and see how they were getting on; and first he went to the gardener's wife. He asked her how she was, and how things were going with herself and her husband. She replied that on the whole they were doing very well: "But," she continued, "I do wish we could have some good heavy rain: the garden wants it badly." Then he went on to the potter's wife and made the same inquiries of her. She replied that she and her husband had nothing to complain of: "But," she went on, "I do wish we could have some nice dry weather, to dry the pottery." Her Father looked at her with a humorous expression on his face. "You want dry weather," he said, "and your sister wants rain. I was going to ask in my prayers that your wishes should be granted; but now it strikes me I had better not refer to the subject."

# 83 :: The Fawn and His Mother

A **Hind** said to her **Fawn**, who was now well grown and strong, "My son, Nature has given you a powerful body and a stout pair of horns, and I can't think why you are such a coward as to run away from the hounds." Just then they both heard the sound of a pack in full cry, but at a considerable distance. "You stay where you are," said the Hind; "never mind me": and with that she ran off as fast as her legs could carry her.

84 :: THE FIR-TREE AND THE BRAMBLE PAGE 62

# 84 :: The Fir-Tree and The Bramble

A Fir-tree was boasting to a **Bramble**, and said, somewhat contemptuously, "You poor creature, you are of no use whatever. Now, look at me: I am useful for all sorts of things, particularly when men build houses; they can't do without me then." But the Bramble replied, "Ah, that's all very well: but you wait till they come with axes and saws to cut you down, and then you'll wish you were a Bramble and not a Fir."

***Better poverty without a care than wealth with its many obligations.***

Proverbs 17: 1
*Better is a dry morsel with quietness,*
*Than a house full of feasting with strife.*

Luke 12: 29
*And do not seek what you should eat or what you should drink, nor have an anxious mind.*

Philippians 4: 6
*Be anxious for nothing, but in everything by prayer and supplication, with thanksgiving, let your requests be made known to God...*

# 85 :: The Fisherman and The Sprat

A Fisherman cast his net into the sea, and when he drew it up again it contained nothing but a single **Sprat** that begged to be put back into the water. "I'm only a little fish now," it said, "but I shall grow big one day, and then if you come and catch me again I shall be of some use to you." But the Fisherman replied, "Oh, no, I shall keep you now I've got you: if I put you back, should I ever see you again? Not likely!"

# 86 :: The Fisherman Piping

A Fisherman who could play the flute went down one day to the sea-shore with his nets and his flute; and, taking his stand on a projecting rock, began to play a tune, thinking that the music would bring the fish jumping out of the sea. He went on playing for some time, but not a fish appeared: so at last he threw down his flute and cast his net into the sea, and made a great haul of fish. When they were landed and he saw them leaping about on the shore, he cried, "You rascals! you wouldn't dance when I piped: but now I've stopped, you can do nothing else!"

# 87 :: The Flea and The Man

A Flea bit a Man, and bit him again, and again, till he could stand it no longer, but made a thorough search for it, and at last succeeded in catching it. Holding it between his finger and thumb, he said—or rather shouted, so angry was he—"Who are you, pray, you wretched little creature, that you make so free with my person?" The Flea, terrified, whimpered in a weak little voice, "Oh, sir! pray let me go; don't kill me! I am such a little thing that I can't do you much harm." But the Man laughed and said, "I am going to kill you now, at once: whatever is bad has got to be destroyed, no matter how slight the harm it does."

***Do not waste your pity on a scamp.***

Proverbs 19: 19
*A man of great wrath shall suffer the penalty; for if you deliver him [from the consequences], he will [feel free to] cause you to do it again. (AMP)*

# 88 :: The Flea and The Ox

A Flea once said to an Ox, "How comes it that a big strong fellow like you is content to serve mankind, and do all their hard work for them, while I, who am no bigger than you see, live on their bodies and drink my fill of their blood, and never do a stroke for it all?" To which the Ox replied, "Men are very kind to me, and so I am grateful to them: they feed and house me well, and every now and then they show their fondness for me by patting me on the head and neck." "They'd pat me, too," said the Flea, "if I let them: but I take good care they don't, or there would be nothing left of me."

# 89 :: The Fly and The Draught-Mule

A Fly sat on one of the shafts of a cart and said to the Mule who was pulling it, "How slow you are! Do mend your pace, or I shall have to use my sting as a goad." The Mule was not in the least disturbed. "Behind me, in the cart," said he, "sits my master. He holds the reins, and flicks me with his whip, and him I obey, but I don't want any of your impertinence. I know when I may dawdle and when I may not."

# 90 :: The Fowler and The Lark

A **Fowler** was setting his nets for little birds when a Lark came up to him and asked him what he was doing. "I am engaged in founding a city," said he, and with that he withdrew a short distance and concealed himself. The Lark examined the nets with great curiosity, and presently, catching sight of the bait, hopped on to them in order to secure it, and became entangled in the meshes. The Fowler then ran up quickly and captured her. "What a fool I was!" said she: "but at any rate, if that's the kind of city you are founding, it'll be a long time before you find fools enough to fill it."

# 91 :: The Fowler, The Partridge, and The Cock

One day, as a **Fowler** was sitting down to a scanty supper of herbs and bread, a friend dropped in unexpectedly. The **larder** was empty; so he went out and caught a tame **Partridge**, which he kept as a decoy, and was about to wring her neck when she cried, "Surely you won't kill me? Why, what will you do without me next time you go fowling? How will you get the birds to come to your nets?" He let her go at this, and went to his hen-house, where he had a plump young **Cock**. When the Cock saw what he was after, he too pleaded for his life, and said, "If you kill me, how will you know the time of night? and who will wake you up in the morning when it is time to get to work?" The Fowler, however, replied, "You are useful for telling the time, I know; but, for all that, I can't send my friend supperless to bed." And therewith he caught him and wrung his neck.

# 92 :: The Fox and The Bramble

In making his way through a hedge a Fox missed his footing and caught at a **Bramble** to save himself from falling. Naturally, he got badly scratched, and in disgust he cried to the Bramble, "It was your help I wanted, and see how you have treated me! I'd sooner have fallen outright." The Bramble, interrupting him, replied, "You must have lost your wits, my friend, to catch at me, who am myself always catching at others."

# 93 :: The Fox and The Crow

A Crow was sitting on a branch of a tree with a piece of cheese in her beak when a Fox observed her and set his wits to work to discover some way of getting the cheese. Coming and standing under the tree he looked up and said, "What a noble bird I see above me! Her beauty is without equal, the hue of her plumage exquisite. If only her voice is as sweet as her looks are fair, she ought without doubt to be Queen of the Birds." The Crow was hugely flattered by this, and just to show the Fox that she could sing she gave a loud caw. Down came the cheese, of course, and the Fox, snatching it up, said, "You have a voice, madam, I see: what you want is wits."

***Flattery finds favor.***

Job 32: 21
*Let me not, I pray, show partiality to anyone;*
*Nor let me flatter any man.*

Proverbs 29: 5
*A man who flatters his neighbor spreads a net for his own feet.*

# 94 :: The Fox and The Goat

A Fox fell into a well and was unable to get out again. By and by a thirsty Goat came by, and seeing the Fox in the well asked him if the water was good. "Good?" said the Fox, "it's the best water I ever tasted in all my life. Come down and try it yourself." The Goat thought of nothing but the prospect of quenching his thirst, and jumped in at once. When he had had enough to drink, he looked about, like the Fox, for some way of getting out, but could find none. Presently the Fox said, "I have an idea. You stand on your hind legs, and plant your forelegs firmly against the side of the well, and then I'll climb on to your back, and, from there, by stepping on your horns, I can get out. And when I'm out, I'll help you out too." The Goat did as he was requested, and the Fox climbed on to his back and so out of the well; and then he coolly walked away. The Goat called loudly after him and reminded him of his promise to help him out: but the Fox merely turned and said, "If you had as much sense in your head as you have hair in your beard you wouldn't have got into the well without making certain that you could get out again."

***Look before you leap.***

Proverbs 24: 6
*For by wise counsel you will wage your own war,*
*And in a multitude of counselors there is safety.*

Isaiah 30: 1
*"Woe to the rebellious children," says the Lord,*
*"Who take counsel, but not of Me,*
*And who devise plans, but not of My Spirit,*
*That they may add sin to sin..."*

93 :: THE FOX AND THE CROW PAGE 67

# 95 :: The Fox and The Grapes

A hungry Fox saw some fine bunches of Grapes hanging from a vine that was trained along a high trellis, and did his best to reach them by jumping as high as he could into the air. But it was all in vain, for they were just out of reach: so he gave up trying, and walked away with an air of dignity and unconcern, remarking, "I thought those Grapes were ripe, but I see now they are quite sour."

# 96 :: The Fox and The Grasshopper

A Grasshopper sat chirping in the branches of a tree. A Fox heard her, and, thinking what a dainty morsel she would make, he tried to get her down by a trick. Standing below in full view of her, he praised her song in the most flattering terms, and begged her to descend, saying he would like to make the acquaintance of the owner of so beautiful a voice. But she was not to be taken in, and replied, "You are very much mistaken, my dear sir, if you imagine I am going to come down: I keep well out of the way of you and your kind ever since the day when I saw numbers of grasshoppers' wings strewn about the entrance to a fox's earth."

# 97 :: The Fox and The Hedgehog

A Fox, in swimming across a rapid river, was swept away by the current and carried a long way downstream in spite of his struggles, until at last, bruised and exhausted, he managed to scramble on to dry ground from a backwater. As he lay there unable to move, a swarm of horseflies settled on him and sucked his blood undisturbed, for he was too weak even to shake them off. A **Hedgehog** saw him, and asked if he should brush away the flies that were tormenting him; but the Fox replied, "Oh, please, no, not on any account, for these flies have sucked their fill and are taking very little from me now; but, if you drive them off, another swarm of hungry ones will come and suck all the blood I have left, and leave me without a drop in my veins."

# 98 :: The Fox and The Leopard

A Fox and a Leopard were disputing about their looks, and each claimed to be the more handsome of the two. The Leopard said, "Look at my smart coat; you have nothing to match that." But the Fox replied, "Your coat may be smart, but my wits are smarter still."

# 99 :: The Fox and The Lion

A Fox who had never seen a Lion one day met one, and was so terrified at the sight of him that he was ready to die with fear. After a time he met him again, and was still rather frightened, but not nearly so much as he had been when he met him first. But when he saw him for the third time he was so far from being afraid that he went up to him and began to talk to him as if he had known him all his life.

# 100 :: The Fox and The Monkey

A Fox and a Monkey were on the road together, and fell into a dispute as to which of the two was the better born. They kept it up for some time, till they came to a place where the road passed through a cemetery full of monuments, when the Monkey stopped and looked about him and gave a great sigh. "Why do you sigh?" said the Fox. The Monkey pointed to the tombs and replied, "All the monuments that you see here were put up in honour of my forefathers, who in their day were eminent men." The Fox was speechless for a moment, but quickly recovering he said, "Oh! don't stop at any lie, sir; you're quite safe: I'm sure none of your ancestors will rise up and expose you."

***Boasters brag most when they cannot be detected.***

James 4: 15-16
*Instead you ought to say, "If the Lord wills, we shall live and do this or that." But now you boast in your arrogance. All such boasting is evil.*

# 101 :: The Fox and The Snake

A Snake, in crossing a river, was carried away by the current, but managed to wriggle onto a bundle of thorns which was floating by, and was thus carried at a great rate down-stream. A Fox caught sight of it from the bank as it went whirling along, and called out, "Gad! the passenger fits the ship!"

# 102 :: The Fox and The Stork

A Fox invited a Stork to dinner, at which the only fare provided was a large flat dish of soup. The Fox lapped it up with great relish, but the **Stork** with her long bill tried in vain to partake of the savoury broth. Her evident distress caused the sly Fox much amusement. But not long after the Stork invited him in turn, and set before him a pitcher with a long and narrow neck, into which she could get her bill with ease. Thus, while she enjoyed her dinner, the Fox sat by hungry and helpless, for it was impossible for him to reach the tempting contents of the vessel.

# 103 :: The Fox Who Served a Lion

A Lion had a Fox to attend on him, and whenever they went hunting the Fox found the prey and the Lion fell upon it and killed it, and then they divided it between them in certain proportions. But the Lion always got a very large share, and the Fox a very small one, which didn't please the latter at all; so he determined to set up on his own account. He began by trying to steal a lamb from a flock of sheep: but the shepherd saw him and set his dogs on him. The hunter was now the hunted, and was very soon caught and despatched by the dogs.

***Better servitude with safety than freedom with danger.***

Luke 3: 14
*...be content with your wages.*

# 104 :: The Fox Without a Tail

A fox once fell into a trap, and after a struggle managed to get free, but with the loss of his brush. He was then so much ashamed of his appearance that he thought life was not worth living unless he could persuade the other Foxes to part with their tails also, and thus divert attention from his own loss. So he called a meeting of all the Foxes, and advised them to cut off their tails: "They're ugly things anyhow," he said, "and besides they're heavy, and it's tiresome to be always carrying them about with you." But one of the other Foxes said, "My friend, if you hadn't lost your own tail, you wouldn't be so keen on getting us to cut off ours."

# 105 :: The Foxes and The River

A number of Foxes assembled on the bank of a river and wanted to drink; but the current was so strong and the water looked so deep and dangerous that they didn't dare to do so, but stood near the edge encouraging one another not to be afraid. At last one of them, to shame the rest, and show how brave he was, said, "I am not a bit frightened! See, I'll step right into the water!" He had no sooner done so than the current swept him off his feet. When the others saw him being carried down-stream they cried, "Don't go and leave us! Come back and show us where we too can drink with safety." But he replied, "I'm afraid I can't yet: I want to go to the seaside, and this current will take me there nicely. When I come back I'll show you with pleasure."

# 106 :: The Frogs' Compaint Against The Sun

Once upon a time the Sun was about to take to himself a wife. The Frogs in terror all raised their voices to the skies, and **Jupiter**, disturbed by the noise, asked them what they were croaking about. They replied, "The Sun is bad enough even while he is single, drying up our marshes with his heat as he does. But what will become of us if he marries and begets other Suns?"

107 :: The Frogs and the Well page 78

# 107 :: The Frogs and The Well

Two Frogs lived together in a marsh. But one hot summer the marsh dried up, and they left it to look for another place to live in: for frogs like damp places if they can get them. By and by they came to a deep well, and one of them looked down into it, and said to the other, "This looks a nice cool place: let us jump in and settle here." But the other, who had a wiser head on his shoulders, replied, "Not so fast, my friend: supposing this well dried up like the marsh, how should we get out again?"

***Think twice before you act.***

Luke 14: 28
*For which of you, intending to build a tower, does not sit down first and count the cost, whether he has enough to finish it.*

Example: Jephthah's rash vow:

Judges 11: 31
*...then it will be that whatever comes out of the doors of my house to meet me, when I return in peace from the people of Ammon, shall surely be the Lord's, and I will offer it up as a burnt offering."*

(Full text: Judges 11: 31-39)

108 :: The Frogs Asking for a King page 79

# 108 :: The Frogs Asking for a King

Time was when the Frogs were discontented because they had no one to rule over them: so they sent a deputation to **Jupiter** to ask him to give them a King. Jupiter, despising the folly of their request, cast a log into the pool where they lived, and said that that should be their King. The Frogs were terrified at first by the splash, and scuttled away into the deepest parts of the pool; but by and by, when they saw that the log remained motionless, one by one they ventured to the surface again, and before long, growing bolder, they began to feel such contempt for it that they even took to sitting upon it. Thinking that a King of that sort was an insult to their dignity, they sent to Jupiter a second time, and begged him to take away the sluggish King he had given them, and to give them another and a better one. Jupiter, annoyed at being pestered in this way, sent a **Stork** to rule over them, who no sooner arrived among them than he began to catch and eat the Frogs as fast as he could.

# 109 :: The Gardener and His Dog

A Gardener's Dog fell into a deep well, from which his master used to draw water for the plants in his garden with a rope and a bucket. Failing to get the Dog out by means of these, the Gardener went down into the well himself in order to fetch him up. But the Dog thought he had come to make sure of drowning him; so he bit his master as soon as he came within reach, and hurt him a good deal, with the result that he left the Dog to his fate and climbed out of the well, remarking, "It serves me quite right for trying to save so determined a suicide."

# 110 :: The Gnat and The Bull

A **Gnat** alighted on one of the horns of a Bull, and remained sitting there for a considerable time. When it had rested sufficiently and was about to fly away, it said to the Bull, "Do you mind if I go now?" The Bull merely raised his eyes and remarked, without interest, "It's all one to me; I didn't notice when you came, and I shan't know when you go away."

***We may often be of more consequence in our own eyes than in the eyes of our neighbours.***

Proverbs 25: 6-7
*Do not exalt yourself in the presence of the king,*
*And do not stand in the place of the great;*
*For it is better that he say to you, "Come up here,"*
*Than that you should be put lower in the presence of the prince,*
*Whom your eyes have seen.*

Matthew 20: 16
*So the last will be first, and the first last. For many are called, but few chosen.*

110 :: The Gnat and The Lion page 82

# 111 :: The Gnat and the Lion

A **Gnat** once went up to a Lion and said, "I am not in the least afraid of you: I don't even allow that you are a match for me in strength. What does your strength amount to after all? That you can scratch with your claws and bite with your teeth—just like a woman in a temper—and nothing more. But I'm stronger than you: if you don't believe it, let us fight and see." So saying, the Gnat sounded his horn, and darted in and bit the Lion on the nose. When the Lion felt the sting, in his haste to crush him he scratched his nose badly, and made it bleed, but failed altogether to hurt the Gnat, which buzzed off in triumph, elated by its victory. Presently, however, it got entangled in a spider's web, and was caught and eaten by the spider, thus falling prey to an insignificant insect after having triumphed over the King of the Beasts.

# 112 :: The Goat and The Vine

A Goat was straying in a vineyard, and began to browse on the tender shoots of a Vine which bore several fine bunches of grapes. "What have I done to you," said the Vine, "that you should harm me thus? Isn't there grass enough for you to feed on? All the same, even if you eat up every leaf I have, and leave me quite bare, I shall produce wine enough to pour over you when you are led to the altar to be sacrificed."

Psalm 7: 16
*His trouble shall return upon his own head,*
*And his violent dealing shall come down on his own crown.*

Psalm 9: 16b
*The wicked is snared in the work of his own hands.*

# 113 :: The Goatherd and The Goat

A **Goatherd** was one day gathering his flock to return to the fold, when one of his goats strayed and refused to join the rest. He tried for a long time to get her to return by calling and whistling to her, but the Goat took no notice of him at all; so at last he threw a stone at her and broke one of her horns. In dismay, he begged her not to tell his master: but she replied, "You silly fellow, my horn would cry aloud even if I held my tongue."

***It's no use trying to hide what can't be hidden.***

Luke 8: 17
*For nothing is secret that will not be revealed, nor anything hidden that will not be known and come to light.*

Hebrews 4: 13
*And there is no creature hidden from His sight, but all things are naked and open to the eyes of Him to whom we must give account.*

# 114 :: The Goatherd and The Wild Goats

A **Goatherd** was tending his goats out at pasture when he saw a number of Wild Goats approach and mingle with his flock. At the end of the day he drove them home and put them all into the pen together. Next day the weather was so bad that he could not take them out as usual: so he kept them at home in the pen, and fed them there. He only gave his own goats enough food to keep them from starving, but he gave the Wild Goats as much as they could eat and more; for he was very anxious for them to stay, and he thought that if he fed them well they wouldn't want to leave him. When the weather improved, he took them all out to pasture again; but no sooner had they got near the hills than the Wild Goats broke away from the flock and scampered off. The Goatherd was very much disgusted at this, and roundly abused them for their ingratitude. "Rascals!" he cried, "to run away like that after the way I've treated you!" Hearing this, one of them turned round and said, "Oh, yes, you treated us all right—too well, in fact; it was just that that put us on our guard. If you treat newcomers like ourselves so much better than your own flock, it's more than likely that, if another lot of strange goats joined yours, we should then be neglected in favour of the last comers."

1 Peter 4: 9
*Be hospitable to one another without grumbling.*

# 115 :: The Goods and Ills

There was a time in the youth of the world when Goods and Ills entered equally into the concerns of men, so that the Goods did not prevail to make them altogether blessed, nor the Ills to make them wholly miserable. But owing to the foolishness of mankind the Ills multiplied greatly in number and increased in strength, until it seemed as though they would deprive the Goods of all share in human affairs, and banish them from the earth. The latter, therefore, betook themselves to heaven and complained to **Jupiter** of the treatment they had received, at the same time praying him to grant them protection from the Ills, and to advise them concerning the manner of their intercourse with men. Jupiter granted their request for protection, and decreed that for the future they should not go among men openly in a body, and so be liable to attack from the hostile Ills, but singly and unobserved, and at infrequent and unexpected intervals. Hence it is that the earth is full of Ills, for they come and go as they please and are never far away; while Goods, alas! come one by one only, and have to travel all the way from heaven, so that they are very seldom seen.

Proverbs 15: 3
*The eyes of the Lord are in every place,*
*Keeping watch on the evil and the good.*

James 1: 17
*Every good gift and every perfect gift is from above, and comes down from the Father of lights, with whom there is no variation or shadow of turning.*

# 116 :: The Goose That Laid The Golden Eggs

A Man and his Wife had the good fortune to possess a Goose which laid a Golden Egg every day. Lucky though they were, they soon began to think they were not getting rich fast enough, and, imagining the bird must be made of gold inside, they decided to kill it in order to secure the whole store of precious metal at once. But when they cut it open they found it was just like any other goose. Thus, they neither got rich all at once, as they had hoped, nor enjoyed any longer the daily addition to their wealth.

***Much wants more and loses all.***

Proverbs 1: 19
*So are the ways of everyone who is greedy for gain;*
*It takes away the life of its owners.*

Proverbs 28: 22
*A man with an evil eye hastens after riches,*
*And does not consider that poverty will come upon him.*

Example: Matthew 19: 21-22
*Jesus said to him, "If you want to be perfect, go, sell what you have and give to the poor, and you will have treasure in heaven; and come, follow Me." But when the young man heard that saying, he went away sorrowful, for he had great possessions.*

# 117 :: The Grasshopper and The Ants

One fine day in winter some Ants were busy drying their store of corn, which had got rather damp during a long spell of rain. Presently up came a Grasshopper and begged them to spare her a few grains, "For," she said, "I'm simply starving." The Ants stopped work for a moment, though this was against their principles. "May we ask," said they, "what you were doing with yourself all last summer? Why didn't you collect a store of food for the winter?" "The fact is," replied the Grasshopper, "I was so busy singing that I hadn't the time." "If you spent the summer singing," replied the Ants, "you can't do better than spend the winter dancing." And they chuckled and went on with their work.

Proverbs 6: 6
*Go to the ant, you sluggard!*
*Consider her ways and be wise...*

Proverbs 30: 25
*The ants are a people not strong,*
*Yet they prepare their food in the summer...*

# 118 :: The Grasshopper and The Owl

An Owl, who lived in a hollow tree, was in the habit of feeding by night and sleeping by day; but her slumbers were greatly disturbed by the chirping of a Grasshopper, who had taken up his abode in the branches. She begged him repeatedly to have some consideration for her comfort, but the Grasshopper, if anything, only chirped the louder. At last the Owl could stand it no longer, but determined to rid herself of the pest by means of a trick. Addressing herself to the Grasshopper, she said in her pleasantest manner, "As I cannot sleep for your song, which, believe me, is as sweet as the notes of Apollo's lyre, I have a mind to taste some nectar, which **Minerva** gave me the other day. Won't you come in and join me?" The Grasshopper was flattered by the praise of his song, and his mouth, too, watered at the mention of the delicious drink, so he said he would be delighted. No sooner had he got inside the hollow where the Owl was sitting than she pounced upon him and ate him up.

# 119 :: The Hare and The Hound

A Hound started a **Hare** from her **form**, and pursued her for some distance; but as she gradually gained upon him, he gave up the chase. A **rustic** who had seen the race met the Hound as he was returning, and taunted him with his defeat. "The little one was too much for you," said he. "Ah, well," said the Hound, "don't forget it's one thing to be running for your dinner, but quite another to be running for your life."

# 120 :: The Hare and The Tortoise

A **Hare** was one day making fun of a Tortoise for being so slow upon his feet. "Wait a bit," said the Tortoise; "I'll run a race with you, and I'll wager that I win." "Oh, well," replied the Hare, who was much amused at the idea, "let's try and see"; and it was soon agreed that the fox should set a course for them, and be the judge. When the time came both started off together, but the Hare was soon so far ahead that he thought he might as well have a rest: so down he lay and fell fast asleep. Meanwhile the Tortoise kept plodding on, and in time reached the goal. At last the Hare woke up with a start, and dashed on at his fastest, but only to find that the Tortoise had already won the race.

***Slow and steady wins the race.***

1 Corinthians 9: 24
*Do you not know that those who run in a race all run, but one receives the prize? Run in such a way that you may obtain it.*

Hebrews 12: 1
*Therefore we also, since we are surrounded by so great a cloud of witnesses, let us lay aside every weight, and the sin which so easily ensnares us, and let us run with endurance the race that is set before us.*

120 :: The Hare and The Tortoise page 91

# 121 :: The Hares and The Frogs

The **Hares** once gathered together and lamented the unhappiness of their lot, exposed as they were to dangers on all sides and lacking the strength and the courage to hold their own. Men, dogs, birds and beasts of prey were all their enemies, and killed and devoured them daily: and sooner than endure such persecution any longer, they one and all determined to end their miserable lives. Thus resolved and desperate, they rushed in a body towards a neighbouring pool, intending to drown themselves. On the bank were sitting a number of Frogs, who, when they heard the noise of the Hares as they ran, with one accord leaped into the water and hid themselves in the depths. Then one of the older Hares who was wiser than the rest cried out to his companions, "Stop, my friends, take heart; don't let us destroy ourselves after all: see, here are creatures who are afraid of us, and who must, therefore, be still more timid than ourselves."

# 122 :: The Hawk, The Kite, and The Pigeons

The Pigeons in a certain dovecote were persecuted by a **Kite**, who every now and then swooped down and carried off one of their number. So they invited a Hawk into the dovecote to defend them against their enemy. But they soon repented of their folly: for the Hawk killed more of them in a day than the Kite had done in a year.

Proverbs 6: 27
*Can a man take fire to his bosom,*
*And his clothes not be burned?*

# 123 :: The Heifer and The Ox

A **Heifer** went up to an Ox, who was straining hard at the plough, and sympathised with him in a rather patronising sort of way on the necessity of his having to work so hard. Not long afterwards there was a festival in the village and every one kept holiday: but, whereas the Ox was turned loose into the pasture, the Heifer was seized and led off to sacrifice. "Ah," said the Ox, with a grim smile, "I see now why you were allowed to have such an idle time: it was because you were always intended for the altar."

# 124 :: The Herdsman and The Lost Bull

A Herdsman was tending his cattle when he missed a young Bull, one of the finest of the herd. He went at once to look for him, but, meeting with no success in his search, he made a vow that, if he should discover the thief, he would sacrifice a calf to **Jupiter**. Continuing his search, he entered a thicket, where he presently espied a lion devouring the lost Bull. Terrified with fear, he raised his hands to heaven and cried, "Great Jupiter, I vowed I would sacrifice a calf to thee if I should discover the thief: but now a full-grown Bull I promise thee if only I myself escape unhurt from his clutches."

# 125 :: The Horse and His Rider

A Young Man, who fancied himself something of a horseman, mounted a Horse which had not been properly broken in, and was exceedingly difficult to control. No sooner did the Horse feel his weight in the saddle than he bolted, and nothing would stop him. A friend of the Rider's met him in the road in his headlong career, and called out, "Where are you off to in such a hurry?" To which he, pointing to the Horse, replied, "I've no idea: ask him."

# 126 :: The Horse and The Ass

A Horse, proud of his fine harness, met an **Ass** on the high-road. As the Ass with his heavy burden moved slowly out of the way to let him pass, the Horse cried out impatiently that he could hardly resist kicking him to make him move faster. The Ass held his peace, but did not forget the other's insolence. Not long afterwards the Horse became broken-winded, and was sold by his owner to a farmer. One day, as he was drawing a dung-cart, he met the Ass again, who in turn derided him and said, "Aha! you never thought to come to this, did you, you who were so proud! Where are all your gay trappings now?"

# 127 :: The Horse and The Groom

There was once a **Groom** who used to spend long hours clipping and combing the Horse of which he had charge, but who daily stole a portion of his allowance of oats, and sold it for his own profit. The Horse gradually got into worse and worse condition, and at last cried to the Groom, "If you really want me to look sleek and well, you must comb me less and feed me more."

# 128 :: The Horse and The Stag

There was once a Horse who used to graze in a meadow which he had all to himself. But one day a **Stag** came into the meadow, and said he had as good a right to feed there as the Horse, and moreover chose all the best places for himself. The Horse, wishing to be revenged upon his unwelcome visitor, went to a man and asked if he would help him to turn out the Stag. "Yes," said the man, "I will by all means; but I can only do so if you let me put a bridle in your mouth and mount on your back." The Horse agreed to this, and the two together very soon turned the Stag out of the pasture: but when that was done, the Horse found to his dismay that in the man he had got a master for good.

# 129 :: The Hound and The Fox

A Hound, roaming in the forest, spied a lion, and being well used to lesser game, gave chase, thinking he would make a fine quarry. Presently the lion perceived that he was being pursued; so, stopping short, he rounded on his pursuer and gave a loud roar. The Hound immediately turned tail and fled. A Fox, seeing him running away, jeered at him and said, "Ho! ho! There goes the coward who chased a lion and ran away the moment he roared!"

# 130 :: The Hound and The Hare

A young Hound started a **Hare**, and, when he caught her up, would at one moment snap at her with his teeth as though he were about to kill her, while at another he would let go his hold and frisk about her, as if he were playing with another dog. At last the Hare said, "I wish you would show yourself in your true colours! If you are my friend, why do you bite me? If you are my enemy, why do you play with me?"

***He is no friend who plays double.***

Example: Judges 16: 18-19
*When Delilah saw that he had told her everything, she sent word to the rulers of the Philistines, "Come back once more; he has told me everything." So the rulers of the Philistines returned with the silver in their hands. Having put him to sleep on her lap, she called a man to shave off the seven braids of his hair, and so began to subdue him. And his strength left him.*

Proverbs 26: 18-19
*Like a madman who throws firebrands, arrows, and death,*
*Is the man who deceives his neighbor, And says, "I was only joking!"*

# 131 :: The Hunter and The Horseman

A Hunter went out after game, and succeeded in catching a **hare**, which he was carrying home with him when he met a man on horseback, who said to him, "You have had some sport I see, sir," and offered to buy it. The Hunter readily agreed; but the Horseman had no sooner got the hare in his hands than he set spurs to his horse and went off at full gallop. The Hunter ran after him for some little distance; but it soon dawned upon him that he had been tricked, and he gave up trying to overtake the Horseman, and, to save his face, called after him as loud as he could, "All right, sir, all right, take your hare: it was meant all along as a present."

# 132 :: The Hunter and The Woodman

A Hunter was searching in the forest for the tracks of a lion, and, catching sight presently of a Woodman engaged in felling a tree, he went up to him and asked him if he had noticed a lion's footprints anywhere about, or if he knew where his den was. The Woodman answered, "If you will come with me, I will show you the lion himself." The Hunter turned pale with fear, and his teeth chattered as he replied, "Oh, I'm not looking for the lion, thanks, but only for his tracks."

# 133 :: The Image-Seller

A certain man made a wooden Image of **Mercury**, and exposed it for sale in the market. As no one offered to buy it, however, he thought he would try to attract a purchaser by proclaiming the virtues of the Image. So he cried up and down the market, "A god for sale! A god for sale! One who'll bring you luck and keep you lucky!" Presently one of the bystanders stopped him and said, "If your god is all you make him out to be, how is it you don't keep him and make the most of him yourself?" "I'll tell you why," replied he; "he brings gain, it is true, but he takes his time about it; whereas I want money at once."

Ecclesiastes 5: 5
*Better not to vow than to vow and not pay.*

# 134 :: The Imposter

A certain man fell ill, and, being in a very bad way, he made a vow that he would sacrifice a hundred oxen to the gods if they would grant him a return to health. Wishing to see how he would keep his vow, they caused him to recover in a short time. Now, he hadn't an ox in the world, so he made a hundred little oxen out of tallow and offered them up on an altar, at the same time saying, "Ye gods, I call you to witness that I have discharged my vow." The gods determined to be even with him, so they sent him a dream, in which he was bidden to go to the sea-shore and fetch a hundred **crowns** which he was to find there. Hastening in great excitement to the shore, he fell in with a band of robbers, who seized him and carried him off to sell as a slave: and when they sold him a hundred **crowns** was the sum he fetched.

***Do not promise more than you can perform.***

Proverbs 17: 18
*A man devoid of understanding shakes hands in a pledge,*
*And becomes surety for his friend.*

# 135 :: The Jackdaw and The Pigeons

A **Jackdaw**, watching some Pigeons in a farmyard, was filled with envy when he saw how well they were fed, and determined to disguise himself as one of them, in order to secure a share of the good things they enjoyed. So he painted himself white from head to foot and joined the flock; and, so long as he was silent, they never suspected that he was not a pigeon like themselves. But one day he was unwise enough to start chattering, when they at once saw through his disguise and pecked him so unmercifully that he was glad to escape and join his own kind again. But the other jackdaws did not recognise him in his white dress, and would not let him feed with them, but drove him away: and so he became a homeless wanderer for his pains.

Example: King Josiah disguises himself when going into battle and is accidentally killed.

2 Chronicles 35: 22-23
*Nevertheless Josiah would not turn his face from him, but disguised himself so that he might fight with him, and did not heed the words of Necho from the mouth of God. So he came to fight in the Valley of Megiddo. And the archers shot King Josiah; and the king said to his servants, "Take me away, for I am severely wounded."*

# 136 :: The Kid and The Wolf

A Kid strayed from the flock and was chased by a Wolf. When he saw he must be caught he turned round and said to the Wolf, "I know, sir, that I can't escape being eaten by you: and so, as my life is bound to be short, I pray you let it be as merry as may be. Will you not play me a tune to dance to before I die?" The Wolf saw no objection to having some music before his dinner: so he took out his pipe and began to play, while the Kid danced before him. Before many minutes were passed the gods who guarded the flock heard the sound and came up to see what was going on. They no sooner clapped eyes on the Wolf than they gave chase and drove him away. As he ran off, he turned and said to the Kid, "It's what I thoroughly deserve: my trade is the butcher's, and I had no business to turn piper to please you."

# 137 :: The Kid on the Housetop

A Kid climbed up on to the roof of an outhouse, attracted by the grass and other things that grew in the thatch; and as he stood there browsing away, he caught sight of a Wolf passing below, and jeered at him because he couldn't reach him. The Wolf only looked up and said, "I hear you, my young friend; but it is not you who mock me, but the roof on which you are standing."

# 138 :: The Kingdom of The Lion

When the Lion reigned over the beasts of the earth he was never cruel or tyrannical, but as gentle and just as a King ought to be. During his reign he called a general assembly of the beasts, and drew up a code of laws under which all were to live in perfect equality and harmony: the Wolf and the Lamb, the Tiger and the **Stag**, the Leopard and the Kid, the Dog and the **Hare**, all should dwell side by side in unbroken peace and friendship. The Hare said, "Oh! how I have longed for this day when the weak take their place without fear by the side of the strong!"

# 139 :: The Labourer and The Snake

A Labourer's little son was bitten by a Snake and died of the wound. The father was beside himself with grief, and in his anger against the Snake he caught up an axe and went and stood close to the Snake's hole, and watched for a chance of killing it. Presently the Snake came out, and the man aimed a blow at it, but only succeeded in cutting off the tip of its tail before it wriggled in again. He then tried to get it to come out a second time, pretending that he wished to make up the quarrel. But the Snake said, "I can never be your friend because of my lost tail, nor you mine because of your lost child."

***Injuries are never forgotten in the presence of those who caused them.***

This fable shows it is human nature to remember an offense. God asks us to be like Himself and forgive.

Proverbs 19: 11
*The discretion of a man makes him slow to anger,*
*And his glory is to overlook a transgression.*

# 140 :: The Lamb Chased by a Wolf

A Wolf was chasing a Lamb, which took refuge in a temple. The Wolf urged it to come out of the precincts, and said, "If you don't, the priest is sure to catch you and offer you up in sacrifice on the altar." To which the Lamb replied, "Thanks, I think I'll stay where I am: I'd rather be sacrificed any day than be eaten up by a Wolf."

# 141 :: The Lamp

A Lamp, well filled with oil, burned with a clear and steady light, and began to swell with pride and boast that it shone more brightly than the sun himself. Just then a puff of wind came and blew it out. Some one struck a match and lit it again, and said, "You just keep alight, and never mind the sun. Why, even the stars never need to be relit as you had to be just now."

# 142 :: The Lark and The Farmer

A Lark nested in a field of corn, and was rearing her brood under cover of the ripening grain. One day, before the young were fully fledged, the Farmer came to look at the crop, and, finding it yellowing fast, he said, "I must send round word to my neighbours to come and help me reap this field." One of the young Larks overheard him, and was very much frightened, and asked her mother whether they hadn't better move house at once. "There's no hurry," replied she; "a man who looks to his friends for help will take his time about a thing." In a few days the Farmer came by again, and saw that the grain was overripe and falling out of the ears upon the ground. "I must put it off no longer," he said; "This very day I'll hire the men and set them to work at once." The Lark heard him and said to her young, "Come, my children, we must be off: he talks no more of his friends now, but is going to take things in hand himself."

***Self-help is the best help.***

Example: Genesis 14: 23
*...that I will take nothing, from a thread to a sandal strap, and that I will not take anything that is yours, lest you should say, "I have made Abram rich..."*

2 Thessalonians 3: 8
*...nor did we eat anyone's bread free of charge, but worked with labor and toil night and day, that we might not be a burden to any of you...*

# 143 :: The Lion and The Ass

A Lion and an **Ass** set up as partners and went a-hunting together. In the course of time they came to a cave in which there were a number of wild goats. The Lion took up his stand at the mouth of the cave, and waited for them to come out; while the Ass went inside and brayed for all he was worth in order to frighten them out into the open. The Lion struck them down one by one as they appeared; and when the cave was empty the Ass came out and said, "Well, I scared them pretty well, didn't I?" "I should think you did," said the Lion: "why, if I hadn't known you were an Ass, I should have turned and run myself."

# 144 :: The Lion and The Boar

One hot and thirsty day in the height of summer a Lion and a **Boar** came down to a little spring at the same moment to drink. In a trice they were quarrelling as to who should drink first. The quarrel soon became a fight and they attacked one another with the utmost fury. Presently, stopping for a moment to take breath, they saw some vultures seated on a rock above evidently waiting for one of them to be killed, when they would fly down and feed upon the carcase. The sight sobered them at once, and they made up their quarrel, saying, "We had much better be friends than fight and be eaten by vultures."

Matthew 5: 25
*Agree with your adversary quickly, while you are on the way with him, lest your adversary deliver you to the judge, the judge hand you over to the officer, and you be thrown into prison.*

# 145 :: The Lion and The Bull

A Lion saw a fine fat Bull pasturing among a herd of cattle and cast about for some means of getting him into his clutches; so he sent him word that he was sacrificing a sheep, and asked if he would do him the honour of dining with him. The Bull accepted the invitation, but, on arriving at the Lion's den, he saw a great array of saucepans and spits, but no sign of a sheep; so he turned on his heel and walked quietly away. The Lion called after him in an injured tone to ask the reason, and the Bull turned round and said, "I have reason enough. When I saw all your preparations it struck me at once that the victim was to be a Bull and not a sheep."

***The net is spread in vain in sight of the bird.***

Psalm 10: 9
*He lies in wait secretly, as a lion in his den;*
*He lies in wait to catch the poor;*
*He catches the poor when he draws him into his net.*

Proverbs 1: 16-17
*For their feet run to evil,*
*And they make haste to shed blood.*
*Surely, in vain the net is spread*
*In the sight of any bird...*

# 146 :: The Lion and The Hare

A Lion found a **Hare** sleeping in her **form**, and was just going to devour her when he caught sight of a passing **stag**. Dropping the Hare, he at once made for the bigger game; but finding, after a long chase, that he could not overtake the stag, he abandoned the attempt and came back for the Hare. When he reached the spot, however, he found she was nowhere to be seen, and he had to go without his dinner. "It serves me right," he said; "I should have been content with what I had got, instead of hankering after a better prize."

## 147 :: THE LION AND THE MOUSE

A LION ASLEEP IN HIS LAIR WAS WAKED UP BY A MOUSE running over his face. Losing his temper he seized it with his paw and was about to kill it. The Mouse, terrified, piteously entreated him to spare its life. "Please let me go," it cried, "and one day I will repay you for your kindness." The idea of so insignificant a creature ever being able to do anything for him amused the Lion so much that he laughed aloud, and good-humouredly let it go. But the Mouse's chance came, after all. One day the Lion got entangled in a net which had been spread for game by some hunters, and the Mouse heard and recognised his roars of anger and ran to the spot. Without more ado it set to work to gnaw the ropes with its teeth, and succeeded before long in setting the Lion free. "There!" said the Mouse, "you laughed at me when I promised I would repay you: but now you see, even a Mouse can help a Lion."

## 148 :: THE LION AND THE THREE BULLS

THREE BULLS WERE GRAZING IN A MEADOW, AND WERE WATCHED BY A LION, who longed to capture and devour them, but who felt that he was no match for the three so long as they kept together. So he began by false whispers and malicious hints to foment jealousies and distrust among them. This stratagem succeeded so well that ere long the Bulls grew cold and unfriendly, and finally avoided each other and fed each one by himself apart. No sooner did the Lion see this than he fell upon them one by one and killed them in turn.

***In union is strength.***

Ecclesiastes 4: 12
*Though one may be overpowered by another, two can withstand him. And a threefold cord is not quickly broken.*

Ecclesiastes 4: 10
*For if they fall, one will lift up his companion. But woe to him who is alone when he falls, for he has no one to help him up.*

# 149 :: The Lion and The Wild Ass

A Lion and a Wild **Ass** went out hunting together: the latter was to run down the prey by his superior speed, and the former would then come up and despatch it. They met with great success; and when it came to sharing the spoil the Lion divided it all into three equal portions. "I will take the first," said he, "because I am King of the beasts; I will also take the second, because, as your partner, I am entitled to half of what remains; and as for the third—well, unless you give it up to me and take yourself off pretty quick, the third, believe me, will make you feel very sorry for yourself!"

***Might makes right.***

Might in God's Kingdom is of a very different kind:

I Sam 2: 9

*For by strength shall no man prevail.*

Luke 22: 27

*For who is greater, he who sits at the table, or he who serves? Is it not he who sits at the table? Yet I am among you as the One who serves.*

2 Corinthians 12: 9

*"My grace is sufficient for you, for my strength is made perfect in weakness."*

# 150 :: The Lion in Love

A Lion fell deeply in love with the daughter of a cottager and wanted to marry her; but her father was unwilling to give her to so fearsome a husband, and yet didn't want to offend the Lion; so he hit upon the following expedient. He went to the Lion and said, "I think you will make a very good husband for my daughter: but I cannot consent to your union unless you let me draw your teeth and pare your nails, for my daughter is terribly afraid of them." The Lion was so much in love that he readily agreed that this should be done. When once, however, he was thus disarmed, the Cottager was afraid of him no longer, but drove him away with his club.

# 151 :: The Lion, Jupiter, and The Elephant

The Lion, for all his size and strength, and his sharp teeth and claws, is a coward in one thing: he can't bear the sound of a **cock** crowing, and runs away whenever he hears it. He complained bitterly to **Jupiter** for making him like that; but Jupiter said it wasn't his fault: he had done the best he could for him, and, considering this was his only failing, he ought to be well content. The Lion, however, wouldn't be comforted, and was so ashamed of his timidity that he wished he might die. In this state of mind, he met the Elephant and had a talk with him. He noticed that the great beast cocked up his ears all the time, as if he were listening for something, and he asked him why he did so. Just then a **gnat** came humming by, and the Elephant said, "Do you see that wretched little buzzing insect? I'm terribly afraid of its getting into my ear: if it once gets in, I'm dead and done for." The Lion's spirits rose at once when he heard this: "For," he said to himself, "if the Elephant, huge as he is, is afraid of a gnat, I needn't be so much ashamed of being afraid of a cock, who is ten thousand times bigger than a gnat."

# 152 :: The Lion, The Bear, and The Fox

A Lion and a Bear were fighting for possession of a kid, which they had both seized at the same moment. The battle was long and fierce, and at length both of them were exhausted, and lay upon the ground severely wounded and gasping for breath. A Fox had all the time been prowling round and watching the fight: and when he saw the combatants lying there too weak to move, he slipped in and seized the kid, and ran off with it. They looked on helplessly, and one said to the other, "Here we've been mauling each other all this while, and no one the better for it except the Fox!"

# 153 :: The Lion, The Fox, and The Ass

A Lion, a Fox, and an **Ass** went out hunting together. They had soon taken a large booty, which the Lion requested the Ass to divide between them. The Ass divided it all into three equal parts, and modestly begged the others to take their choice; at which the Lion, bursting with fury, sprang upon the Ass and tore him to pieces. Then, glaring at the Fox, he bade him make a fresh division. The Fox gathered almost the whole in one great heap for the Lion's share, leaving only the smallest possible morsel for himself. "My dear friend," said the Lion, "how did you get the knack of it so well?" The Fox replied, "Me? Oh, I took a lesson from the Ass."

***Happy is he who learns from the misfortunes of others.***

Proverbs 1: 5
*A wise man will hear and increase learning,*
*And a man of understanding will attain wise counsel.*

# 154 :: The Lion, The Fox, and The Stag

A Lion lay sick in his den, unable to provide himself with food. So he said to his friend the Fox, who came to ask how he did, "My good friend, I wish you would go to yonder wood and beguile the big **Stag**, who lives there, to come to my den: I have a fancy to make my dinner off a stag's heart and brains." The Fox went to the wood and found the Stag and said to him, "My dear sir, you're in luck. You know the Lion, our King: well, he's at the point of death, and has appointed you his successor to rule over the beasts. I hope you won't forget that I was the first to bring you the good news. And now I must be going back to him; and, if you take my advice, you'll come too and be with him at the last." The Stag was highly flattered, and followed the Fox to the Lion's den, suspecting nothing. No sooner had he got inside than the Lion sprang upon him, but he misjudged his spring, and the Stag got away with only his ears torn, and returned as fast as he could to the shelter of the wood. The Fox was much mortified, and the Lion, too, was dreadfully disappointed, for he was getting very hungry in spite of his illness. So he begged the Fox to have another try at coaxing the Stag to his den. "It'll be almost impossible this time," said the Fox, "but I'll try"; and off he went to the wood a second time, and found the Stag resting and trying to recover from his fright. As soon as he saw the Fox he cried, "You scoundrel, what do you mean by trying to lure me to my death like that? Take yourself off, or I'll do you to death with my horns." But the Fox was entirely shameless. "What a coward you were," said he; "surely you didn't think the Lion meant any harm? Why, he was only going to whisper some royal secrets into your ear when you went off like a scared rabbit. You have rather disgusted him, and I'm not sure he won't make the wolf King instead, unless you come back at once and show you've got some spirit. I promise you he won't hurt you, and I will be your faithful servant." The Stag was foolish enough to be persuaded to return, and this time the Lion made no mistake, but overpowered him, and feasted right royally upon his carcase. The Fox, meanwhile, watched his chance and, when the Lion wasn't looking, filched away the brains to reward him for his trouble. Presently the Lion began searching for them, of course without success: and the Fox, who was watching him, said, "I don't think it's much use your looking for the brains: a creature who twice walked into a Lion's den can't have got any."

151 :: THE LION, JUPITER, AND THE ELEPHANT PAGE 109

# 155 :: The Lion, The Mouse, and The Fox

A Lion was lying asleep at the mouth of his den when a Mouse ran over his back and tickled him so that he woke up with a start and began looking about everywhere to see what it was that had disturbed him. A Fox, who was looking on, thought he would have a joke at the expense of the Lion; so he said, "Well, this is the first time I've seen a Lion afraid of a Mouse." "Afraid of a Mouse?" said the Lion testily: "not I! It's his bad manners I can't stand."

# 156 :: The Lion, The Wolf, and The Fox

A Lion, infirm with age, lay sick in his den, and all the beasts of the forest came to inquire after his health with the exception of the Fox. The Wolf thought this was a good opportunity for paying off old scores against the Fox, so he called the attention of the Lion to his absence, and said, "You see, sire, that we have all come to see how you are except the Fox, who hasn't come near you, and doesn't care whether you are well or ill." Just then the Fox came in and heard the last words of the Wolf. The Lion roared at him in deep displeasure, but he begged to be allowed to explain his absence, and said, "Not one of them cares for you so much as I, sire, for all the time I have been going round to the doctors and trying to find a cure for your illness." "And may I ask if you have found one?" said the Lion. "I have, sire," said the Fox, "and it is this: you must flay a Wolf and wrap yourself in his skin while it is still warm." The Lion accordingly turned to the Wolf and struck him dead with one blow of his paw, in order to try the Fox's prescription; but the Fox laughed and said to himself, "That's what comes of stirring up ill-will."

# 157 :: The Lioness and The Vixen

A Lioness and a **Vixen** were talking together about their young, as mothers will, and saying how healthy and well-grown they were, and what beautiful coats they had, and how they were the image of their parents. "My litter of cubs is a joy to see," said the Fox; and then she added, rather maliciously, "But I notice you never have more than one." "No," said the Lioness grimly, "but that one's a lion."

***Quality, not quantity.***

Example: 1 Samuel 17: 45-46
*Then David said to the Philistine [Goliath], "You come to me with a sword, with a spear, and with a javelin. But I come to you in the name of the Lord of hosts, the God of the armies of Israel, whom you have defied. This day the Lord will deliver you into my hand, and I will strike you and take your head from you..."*

1 Corinthians 12: 31
*But earnestly desire the best gifts. And yet I show you a more excellent way.*

# 158 :: The Man and His Two Sweethearts

A Man of middle age, whose hair was turning grey, had two Sweethearts, an old woman and a young one. The elder of the two didn't like having a lover who looked so much younger than herself; so, whenever he came to see her, she used to pull the dark hairs out of his head to make him look old. The younger, on the other hand, didn't like him to look so much older than herself, and took every opportunity of pulling out the grey hairs, to make him look young. Between them, they left not a hair in his head, and he became perfectly bald.

# 159 :: The Man and The Image

A poor Man had a wooden Image of a god, to which he used to pray daily for riches. He did this for a long time, but remained as poor as ever, till one day he caught up the Image in disgust and hurled it with all his strength against the wall. The force of the blow split open the head and a quantity of gold coins fell out upon the floor. The Man gathered them up greedily, and said, "O you old fraud, you! When I honoured you, you did me no good whatever: but no sooner do I treat you to insults and violence than you make a rich man of me!"

# 160 :: The Man and The Lion

A Man and a Lion were companions on a journey, and in the course of conversation they began to boast about their prowess, and each claimed to be superior to the other in strength and courage. They were still arguing with some heat when they came to a cross-road where there was a statue of a Man strangling a Lion. "There!" said the Man triumphantly, "look at that! Doesn't that prove to you that we are stronger than you?" "Not so fast, my friend," said the Lion: "that is only your view of the case. If we Lions could make statues, you may be sure that in most of them you would see the Man underneath."

***There are two sides to every question.***

Proverbs 25: 2
*It is the glory of God to conceal a matter,*
*But the glory of kings is to search out a matter.*

# 161 :: The Man and The Satyr

A Man and a **Satyr** became friends, and determined to live together. All went well for a while, until one day in winter-time the Satyr saw the Man blowing on his hands. "Why do you do that?" he asked. "To warm my hands," said the Man. That same day, when they sat down to supper together, they each had a steaming hot bowl of porridge, and the Man raised his bowl to his mouth and blew on it. "Why do you do that?" asked the Satyr. "To cool my porridge," said the Man. The Satyr got up from the table. "Good-bye," said he, "I'm going: I can't be friends with a man who blows hot and cold with the same breath."

161 :: The Man and The Satyr page 115

# 162 :: The Man Who Lost His Spade

A Man was engaged in digging over his vineyard, and one day on coming to work he missed his Spade. Thinking it may have been stolen by one of his labourers, he questioned them closely, but they one and all denied any knowledge of it. He was not convinced by their denials, and insisted that they should all go to the town and take oath in a temple that they were not guilty of the theft. This was because he had no great opinion of the simple country deities, but thought that the thief would not pass undetected by the shrewder gods of the town. When they got inside the gates the first thing they heard was the town crier proclaiming a reward for information about a thief who had stolen something from the city temple. "Well," said the Man to himself, "it strikes me I had better go back home again. If these town gods can't detect the thieves who steal from their own temples, it's scarcely likely they can tell me who stole my Spade."

174 :: The Moon and Her Mother page 129

# 163 :: The Man, The Horse, The Ox, and The Dog

One winter's day, during a severe storm, a Horse, an Ox, and a Dog came and begged for shelter in the house of a Man. He readily admitted them, and, as they were cold and wet, he lit a fire for their comfort: and he put oats before the Horse, and hay before the Ox, while he fed the Dog with the remains of his own dinner. When the storm abated, and they were about to depart, they determined to show their gratitude in the following way. They divided the life of Man among them, and each endowed one part of it with the qualities which were peculiarly his own. The Horse took youth, and hence young men are high-mettled and impatient of restraint; the Ox took middle age, and accordingly men in middle life are steady and hard-working; while the Dog took old age, which is the reason why old men are so often peevish and ill-tempered, and, like dogs, attached chiefly to those who look to their comfort, while they are disposed to snap at those who are unfamiliar or distasteful to them.

# 164 :: The Mice and The Weasels

There was war between the Mice and the Weasels, in which the Mice always got the worst of it, numbers of them being killed and eaten by the Weasels. So they called a council of war, in which an old Mouse got up and said, "It's no wonder we are always beaten, for we have no generals to plan our battles and direct our movements in the field." Acting on his advice, they chose the biggest Mice to be their leaders, and these, in order to be distinguished from the rank and file, provided themselves with helmets bearing large plumes of straw. They then led out the Mice to battle, confident of victory: but they were defeated as usual, and were soon scampering as fast as they could to their holes. All made their way to safety without difficulty except the leaders, who were so hampered by the badges of their rank that they could not get into their holes, and fell easy victims to their pursuers.

***Greatness carries its own penalties.***

Example: Genesis 37: 5-8
*Now Joseph had a dream, and he told it to his brothers; and they hated him even more. So he said to them, "Please hear this dream which I have dreamed: There we were, binding sheaves in the field. Then behold, my sheaf arose and also stood upright; and indeed your sheaves stood all around and bowed down to my sheaf." And his brothers said to him, "Shall you indeed reign over us? Or shall you indeed have dominion over us?" So they hated him even more for his dreams and for his words.*

James 5: 1-2
*Come now, you rich, weep and howl for your miseries that are coming upon you! Your riches are corrupted, and your garments are moth-eaten.*

# 165 :: The Mice in Council

Once upon a time all the Mice met together in Council, and discussed the best means of securing themselves against the attacks of the cat. After several suggestions had been debated, a Mouse of some standing and experience got up and said, "I think I have hit upon a plan which will ensure our safety in the future, provided you approve and carry it out. It is that we should fasten a bell round the neck of our enemy the cat, which will by its tinkling warn us of her approach." This proposal was warmly applauded, and it had been already decided to adopt it, when an old Mouse got upon his feet and said, "I agree with you all that the plan before us is an admirable one: but may I ask who is going to bell the cat?"

Deuteronomy 31: 6
*Be strong and of good courage, do not fear nor be afraid of them; for the Lord your God, He is the One who goes with you. He will not leave you nor forsake you.*

Isaiah 41: 6
*Everyone helped his neighbor, And said to his brother, "Be of good courage!"*

# 166 :: The Milkmaid and Her Pail

A farmer's daughter had been out to milk the cows, and was returning to the dairy carrying her pail of milk upon her head. As she walked along, she fell a-musing after this fashion: "The milk in this pail will provide me with cream, which I will make into butter and take to market to sell. With the money I will buy a number of eggs, and these, when hatched, will produce chickens, and by and by I shall have quite a large poultry-yard. Then I shall sell some of my fowls, and with the money which they will bring in I will buy myself a new gown, which I shall wear when I go to the fair; and all the young fellows will admire it, and come and make love to me, but I shall toss my head and have nothing to say to them." Forgetting all about the pail, and suiting the action to the word, she tossed her head. Down went the pail, all the milk was spilled, and all her fine castles in the air vanished in a moment!

***Do not count your chickens before they are hatched.***

James 4: 13-15
*Come now, you who say, "Today or tomorrow we will go to such and such a city, spend a year there, buy and sell, and make a profit"; whereas you do not know what will happen tomorrow. For what is your life? It is even a vapor that appears for a little time and then vanishes away. Instead you ought to say, "If the Lord wills, we shall live and do this or that."*

# 167 :: The Miller, His Son, and Their Ass

A **Miller**, accompanied by his young Son, was driving his **Ass** to market in hopes of finding a purchaser for him. On the road they met a troop of girls, laughing and talking, who exclaimed, "Did you ever see such a pair of fools? To be trudging along the dusty road when they might be riding!" The Miller thought there was sense in what they said; so he made his Son mount the Ass, and himself walked at the side. Presently they met some of his old cronies, who greeted them and said, "You'll spoil that Son of yours, letting him ride while you toil along on foot! Make him walk, young lazybones! It'll do him all the good in the world." The Miller followed their advice, and took his Son's place on the back of the Ass while the boy trudged along behind. They had not gone far when they overtook a party of women and children, and the Miller heard them say, "What a selfish old man! He himself rides in comfort, but lets his poor little boy follow as best he can on his own legs!" So he made his Son get up behind him. Further along the road

they met some travellers, who asked the Miller whether the Ass he was riding was his own property, or a beast hired for the occasion. He replied that it was his own, and that he was taking it to market to sell. "Good heavens!" said they, "with a load like that the poor beast will be so exhausted by the time he gets there that no one will look at him. Why, you'd do better to carry him!" "Anything to please you," said the old man, "we can but try." So they got off, tied the Ass's legs together with a rope and slung him on a pole, and at last reached the town, carrying him between them. This was so absurd a sight that the people ran out in crowds to laugh at it, and chaffed the Father and Son unmercifully, some even calling them lunatics. They had then got to a bridge over the river, where the Ass, frightened by the noise and his unusual situation, kicked and struggled till he broke the ropes that bound him, and fell into the water and was drowned. Whereupon the unfortunate Miller, vexed and ashamed, made the best of his way home again, convinced that in trying to please all he had pleased none, and had lost his Ass into the bargain.

Ephesians 6: 6

*...not with eye service, as men-pleasers, but as bondservants of Christ, doing the will of God from the heart.*

# 168 :: The Mischievous Dog

There was once a Dog who used to snap at people and bite them without any provocation, and who was a great nuisance to every one who came to his master's house. So his master fastened a bell round his neck to warn people of his presence. The Dog was very proud of the bell, and strutted about tinkling it with immense satisfaction. But an old dog came up to him and said, "The fewer airs you give yourself the better, my friend. You don't think, do you, that your bell was given you as a reward of merit? On the contrary, it is a badge of disgrace."

***Notoriety is often mistaken for fame.***

Example Esther 6: 6
*So Haman came in, and the king asked him, "What shall be done for the man whom the king delights to honor?"*
*Now Haman thought in his heart, "Whom would the king delight to honor more than me?"*

Esther 7: 10
*So they hanged Haman on the gallows that he had prepared for Mordecai. Then the king's wrath subsided.*

# 169 :: The Miser

A **Miser** sold everything he had, and melted down his hoard of gold into a single lump, which he buried secretly in a field. Every day he went to look at it, and would sometimes spend long hours gloating over his treasure. One of his men noticed his frequent visits to the spot, and one day watched him and discovered his secret. Waiting his opportunity, he went one night and dug up the gold and stole it. Next day the Miser visited the place as usual, and, finding his treasure gone, fell to tearing his hair and groaning over his loss. In this condition he was seen by one of his neighbours, who asked him what his trouble was. The Miser told him of his misfortune; but the other replied, "Don't take it so much to heart, my friend; put a brick into the hole, and take a look at it every day: you won't be any worse off than before, for even when you had your gold it was of no earthly use to you."

Matthew 25: 24-27
*Then he who had received the one talent came and said, 'Lord, I knew you to be a hard man, reaping where you have not sown, and gathering where you have not scattered seed. And I was afraid, and went and hid your talent in the ground. Look, there you have what is yours.'*

*But his lord answered and said to him, 'You wicked and lazy servant, you knew that I reap where I have not sown, and gather where I have not scattered seed. So you ought to have deposited my money with the bankers, and at my coming I would have received back my own with interest.*

# 170 :: The Mistress and Her Servants

A Widow, thrifty and industrious, had two servants, whom she kept pretty hard at work. They were not allowed to lie long abed in the mornings, but the old lady had them up and doing as soon as the **cock** crew. They disliked intensely having to get up at such an hour, especially in winter-time: and they thought that if it were not for the cock waking up their Mistress so horribly early, they could sleep longer. So they caught it and wrung its neck. But they weren't prepared for the consequences. For what happened was that their Mistress, not hearing the cock crow as usual, waked them up earlier than ever, and set them to work in the middle of the night.

172 :: The Monkey and The Dolphin page 128

# 171 :: The Monkey and The Camel

At a gathering of all the beasts the Monkey gave an exhibition of dancing and entertained the company vastly. There was great applause at the finish, which excited the envy of the Camel and made him desire to win the favour of the assembly by the same means. So he got up from his place and began dancing, but he cut such a ridiculous figure as he plunged about, and made such a grotesque exhibition of his ungainly person, that the beasts all fell upon him with ridicule and drove him away.

Ecclesiastes 4: 4
*Again, I saw that for all toil and every skillful work*
*a man is envied by his neighbor.*
*This also is vanity and grasping for the wind.*

# 172 :: The Monkey and The Dolphin

When people go on a voyage they often take with them lap-dogs or monkeys as pets to wile away the time. Thus it fell out that a man returning to Athens from the East had a pet Monkey on **board** with him. As they neared the coast of Attica a great storm burst upon them, and the ship capsized. All on board were thrown into the water, and tried to save themselves by swimming, the Monkey among the rest. A Dolphin saw him, and, supposing him to be a man, took him on his back and began swimming towards the shore. When they got near the **Piraeus**, which is the port of Athens, the Dolphin asked the Monkey if he was an Athenian. The Monkey replied that he was, and added that he came of a very distinguished family. "Then, of course, you know the Piraeus," continued the Dolphin. The Monkey thought he was referring to some high official or other, and replied, "Oh, yes, he's a very old friend of mine." At that, detecting his hypocrisy, the Dolphin was so disgusted that he dived below the surface, and the unfortunate Monkey was quickly drowned.

# 173 :: The Monkey as King

At a gathering of all the animals the Monkey danced and delighted them so much that they made him their King. The Fox, however, was very much disgusted at the promotion of the Monkey: so having one day found a trap with a piece of meat in it, he took the Monkey there and said to him, "Here is a dainty morsel I have found, sire; I did not take it myself, because I thought it ought to be reserved for you, our King. Will you be pleased to accept it?" The Monkey made at once for the meat and got caught in the trap. Then he bitterly reproached the Fox for leading him into danger; but the Fox only laughed and said, "O Monkey, you call yourself King of the Beasts and haven't more sense than to be taken in like that!"

# 174 :: The Moon and Her Mother

The Moon once begged her Mother to make her a gown. "How can I?" replied she; "there's no fitting your figure. At one time you're a New Moon, and at another you're a Full Moon; and between whiles you're neither one nor the other."

# 175 :: The Mouse and The Bull

A Bull gave chase to a Mouse which had bitten him in the nose: but the Mouse was too quick for him and slipped into a hole in a wall. The Bull charged furiously into the wall again and again until he was tired out, and sank down on the ground exhausted with his efforts. When all was quiet, the Mouse darted out and bit him again. Beside himself with rage he started to his feet, but by that time the Mouse was back in his hole again, and he could do nothing but bellow and fume in helpless anger. Presently he heard a shrill little voice say from inside the wall, "You big fellows don't always have it your own way, you see: sometimes we little ones come off best."

***The battle is not always to the strong.***

Example: 1 Samuel 17: 45-46
*Then David said to the Philistine [Goliath], "You come to me with a sword, with a spear, and with a javelin. But I come to you in the name of the Lord of hosts, the God of the armies of Israel, whom you have defied. This day the Lord will deliver you into my hand, and I will strike you and take your head from you."*

2 Corinthians 12: 10
*Therefore I take pleasure in infirmities, in reproaches, in needs, in persecutions, in distresses, for Christ's sake. For when I am weak, then I am strong.*

# 176 :: The Mouse, The Frog, and The Hawk

A Mouse and a Frog struck up a friendship; they were not well mated, for the Mouse lived entirely on land, while the Frog was equally at home on land or in the water. In order that they might never be separated, the Frog tied himself and the Mouse together by the leg with a piece of thread. As long as they kept on dry land all went fairly well; but, coming to the edge of a pool, the Frog jumped in, taking the Mouse with him, and began swimming about and croaking with pleasure. The unhappy Mouse, however, was soon drowned, and floated about on the surface in the wake of the Frog. There he was spied by a Hawk, who pounced down on him and seized him in his talons. The Frog was unable to loose the knot which bound him to the Mouse, and thus was carried off along with him and eaten by the Hawk.

# 177 :: The Mule

One morning a Mule, who had too much to eat and too little to do, began to think himself a very fine fellow indeed, and frisked about saying, "My father was undoubtedly a high-spirited horse and I take after him entirely." But very soon afterwards he was put into the harness and compelled to go a very long way with a heavy load behind him. At the end of the day, exhausted by his unusual exertions, he said dejectedly to himself, "I must have been mistaken about my father; he can only have been an **ass** after all."

# 178 :: The Nightingale and The Hawk

A **Nightingale** was sitting on a bough of an oak and singing, as her custom was. A hungry Hawk presently spied her, and darting to the spot seized her in his talons. He was just about to tear her in pieces when she begged him to spare her life: "I'm not big enough," she pleaded, "to make you a good meal: you ought to seek your prey among the bigger birds." The Hawk eyed her with some contempt. "You must think me very simple," said he, "if you suppose I am going to give up a certain prize on the chance of a better of which I see at present no signs."

# 179 :: The Nightingale and The Swallow

A Swallow, conversing with a **Nightingale**, advised her to quit the leafy coverts where she made her home, and to come and live with men, like herself, and nest under the shelter of their roofs. But the Nightingale replied, "Time was when I too, like yourself, lived among men: but the memory of the cruel wrongs I then suffered makes them hateful to me, and never again will I approach their dwellings."

***The scene of past sufferings revives painful memories.***

Psalm 137: 1-3
*By the rivers of Babylon,*
*There we sat down, yea, we wept*
*When we remembered Zion.*
*We hung our harps*
*Upon the willows in the midst of it.*
*For there those who carried us away captive asked of us a song,*
*And those who plundered us requested mirth,*
*Saying, "Sing us one of the songs of Zion!"*

180 :: The North Wind and The Sun page 133

# 180 :: The North Wind and The Sun

A dispute arose between the North Wind and the Sun, each claiming that he was stronger than the other. At last they agreed to try their powers upon a traveller, to see which could soonest strip him of his cloak. The North Wind had the first try; and, gathering up all his force for the attack, he came whirling furiously down upon the man, and caught up his cloak as though he would wrest it from him by one single effort: but the harder he blew, the more closely the man wrapped it round himself. Then came the turn of the Sun. At first he beamed gently upon the traveller, who soon unclasped his cloak and walked on with it hanging loosely about his shoulders: then he shone forth in his full strength, and the man, before he had gone many steps, was glad to throw his cloak right off and complete his journey more lightly clad.

***Persuasion is better than force.***

Proverbs 15: 1
*A soft answer turns away wrath,*
*But a harsh word stirs up anger.*

Proverbs 19: 22
*What is desired in a man is kindness,*
*And a poor man is better than a liar.*

# 181 :: The Oak and The Reeds

An Oak that grew on the bank of a river was uprooted by a severe gale of wind, and thrown across the stream. It fell among some Reeds growing by the water, and said to them, "How is it that you, who are so frail and slender, have managed to weather the storm, whereas I, with all my strength, have been torn up by the roots and hurled into the river?" "You were stubborn," came the reply, "and fought against the storm, which proved stronger than you: but we bow and yield to every breeze, and thus the gale passed harmlessly over our heads."

181 :: The Oak and The Reeds page 133

# 182 :: The Old Hound

A Hound who had served his master well for years, and had run down many a quarry in his time, began to lose his strength and speed owing to age. One day, when out hunting, his master started a powerful wild **boar** and set the Hound at him. The latter seized the beast by the ear, but his teeth were gone and he could not retain his hold; so the boar escaped. His master began to scold him severely, but the Hound interrupted him with these words: "My will is as strong as ever, master, but my body is old and feeble. You ought to honour me for what I have been instead of abusing me for what I am."

# 183 :: The Old Lion

A Lion, enfeebled by age and no longer able to procure food for himself by force, determined to do so by cunning. Betaking himself to a cave, he lay down inside and feigned to be sick: and whenever any of the other animals entered to inquire after his health, he sprang upon them and devoured them. Many lost their lives in this way, till one day a Fox called at the cave, and, having a suspicion of the truth, addressed the Lion from outside instead of going in, and asked him how he did. He replied that he was in a very bad way: "But," said he, "why do you stand outside? Pray come in." "I should have done so," answered the Fox, "if I hadn't noticed that all the footprints point towards the cave and none the other way."

# 184 :: The Old Man and Death

An Old Man cut himself a bundle of **faggots** in a wood and started to carry them home. He had a long way to go, and was tired out before he had got much more than half-way. Casting his burden on the ground, he called upon Death to come and release him from his life of toil. The words were scarcely out of his mouth when, much to his dismay, Death stood before him and professed his readiness to serve him. He was almost frightened out of his wits, but he had enough presence of mind to stammer out, "Good sir, if you'd be so kind, pray help me up with my burden again."

# 185 :: The Old Woman and The Doctor

An Old Woman became almost totally blind from a disease of the eyes, and, after consulting a Doctor, made an agreement with him in the presence of witnesses that she should pay him a high fee if he cured her, while if he failed he was to receive nothing. The Doctor accordingly prescribed a course of treatment, and every time he paid her a visit he took away with him some article out of the house, until at last, when he visited her for the last time, and the cure was complete, there was nothing left. When the Old Woman saw that the house was empty she refused to pay him his fee; and, after repeated refusals on her part, he sued her before the magistrates for payment of her debt. On being brought into court she was ready with her defence. "The claimant," said she, "has stated the facts about our agreement correctly. I undertook to pay him a fee if he cured me, and he, on his part, promised to charge nothing if he failed. Now, he says I am cured; but I say that I am blinder than ever, and I can prove what I say. When my eyes were bad I could at any rate see well enough to be aware that my house contained a certain amount of furniture and other things; but now, when according to him I am cured, I am entirely unable to see anything there at all."

# 186 :: The Old Woman and The Wine-Jar

An old Woman picked up an empty Wine-jar which had once contained a rare and costly wine, and which still retained some traces of its exquisite bouquet. She raised it to her nose and sniffed at it again and again. "Ah," she cried, "how delicious must have been the liquid which has left behind so ravishing a smell."

# 187 :: The Olive-Tree and The Fig-Tree

An Olive-tree taunted a Fig-tree with the loss of her leaves at a certain season of the year. "You," she said, "lose your leaves every autumn, and are bare till the spring: whereas I, as you see, remain green and flourishing all the year round." Soon afterwards there came a heavy fall of snow, which settled on the leaves of the Olive so that she bent and broke under the weight; but the flakes fell harmlessly through the bare branches of the Fig, which survived to bear many another crop.

# 188 :: The Owl and The Birds

The Owl is a very wise bird; and once, long ago, when the first oak sprouted in the forest, she called all the other Birds together and said to them, "You see this tiny tree? If you take my advice, you will destroy it now when it is small: for when it grows big, the mistletoe will appear upon it, from which birdlime will be prepared for your destruction." Again, when the first flax was sown, she said to them, "Go and eat up that seed, for it is the seed of the flax, out of which men will one day make nets to catch you." Once more, when she saw the first archer, she warned the Birds that he was their deadly enemy, who would wing his arrows with their own feathers and shoot them. But they took no notice of what she said: in fact, they thought she was rather mad, and laughed at her. When, however, everything turned out as she had foretold, they changed their minds and conceived a great respect for her wisdom. Hence, whenever she appears, the Birds attend upon her in the hope of hearing something that may be for their good. She, however, gives them advice no longer, but sits moping and pondering on the folly of her kind.

Ecclesiastes 2: 13
*Then I saw that wisdom excels folly*
*As light excels darkness.*

188 :: THE OWL AND THE BIRDS PAGE 138

# 189 :: The Ox and The Frog

Two little Frogs were playing about at the edge of a pool when an Ox came down to the water to drink, and by accident trod on one of them and crushed the life out of him. When the old Frog missed him, she asked his brother where he was. "He is dead, mother," said the little Frog; "an enormous big creature with four legs came to our pool this morning and trampled him down in the mud." "Enormous, was he? Was he as big as this?" said the Frog, puffing herself out to look as big as possible. "Oh! yes, much bigger," was the answer. The Frog puffed herself out still more. "Was he as big as this?" said she. "Oh! yes, yes, Mother, MUCH bigger," said the little Frog. And yet again she puffed and puffed herself out till she was almost as round as a ball. "As big as...?" she began—but then she burst.

# 190 :: The Oxen and The Axletrees

A pair of Oxen were drawing a heavily loaded waggon along the highway, and, as they tugged and strained at the yoke, the **Axletrees** creaked and groaned terribly. This was too much for the Oxen, who turned round indignantly and said, "Hullo, you there! Why do you make such a noise when we do all the work?"

***They complain most who suffer least.***

Example of the Israelites in the desert complaining they do not have enough food when they have the Presence of the Lord to lead them:

Numbers 14: 2
*And all the children of Israel complained against Moses and Aaron, and the whole congregation said to them, "If only we had died in the land of Egypt! Or if only we had died in this wilderness!"*

# 191 :: The Oxen and The Butchers

Once upon a time the Oxen determined to be revenged upon the Butchers for the havoc they wrought in their ranks, and plotted to put them to death on a given day. They were all gathered together discussing how best to carry out the plan, and the more violent of them were engaged in sharpening their horns for the fray, when an old Ox got up upon his feet and said, "My brothers, you have good reason, I know, to hate these Butchers, but, at any rate, they understand their trade and do what they have to do without causing unnecessary pain. But if we kill them, others, who have no experience, will be set to slaughter us, and will by their bungling inflict great sufferings upon us. For you may be sure that, even though all the Butchers perish, mankind will never go without their beef."

# 192 :: The Pack-Ass and The Wild Ass

A Wild **Ass**, who was wandering idly about, one day came upon a Pack-ass lying at full length in a sunny spot and thoroughly enjoying himself. Going up to him, he said, "What a lucky beast you are! Your sleek coat shows how well you live: how I envy you!" Not long after the Wild Ass saw his acquaintance again, but this time he was carrying a heavy load, and his driver was following behind and beating him with a thick stick. "Ah, my friend," said the Wild Ass, "I don't envy you any more: for I see you pay dear for your comforts."

***Advantages that are dearly bought are doubtful blessings.***

Proverbs 17: 1
*Better is a dry morsel with quietness,*
*Than a house full of feasting with strife.*

# 193 :: The Pack-Ass, The Wild Ass, and The Lion

A Wild **Ass** saw a Pack-ass jogging along under a heavy load, and taunted him with the condition of slavery in which he lived, in these words: "What a vile lot is yours compared with mine! I am free as the air, and never do a stroke of work; and, as for fodder, I have only to go to the hills and there I find far more than enough for my needs. But you! you depend on your master for food, and he makes you carry heavy loads every day and beats you unmercifully." At that moment a Lion appeared on the scene, and made no attempt to molest the Pack-ass owing to the presence of the driver; but he fell upon the Wild Ass, who had no one to protect him, and without more ado made a meal of him.

***It is no use being your own master unless you can stand up for yourself.***

Example: Genesis 14: 22-24
*But Abram said to the king of Sodom, "I have raised my hand to the Lord, God Most High, the Possessor of heaven and earth, that I will take nothing, from a thread to a sandal strap, and that I will not take anything that is yours, lest you should say, 'I have made Abram rich'— except only what the young men have eaten, and the portion of the men who went with me..."*

1 Thessalonians 2: 9
*For you remember, brethren, our labor and toil; for laboring night and day, that we might not be a burden to any of you, we preached to you the gospel of God.*

# 194 :: The Parrot and The Cat

A Man once bought a Parrot and gave it the run of his house. It revelled in its liberty, and presently flew up on to the mantelpiece and screamed away to its heart's content. The noise disturbed the Cat, who was asleep on the hearthrug. Looking up at the intruder, she said, "Who may you be, and where have you come from?" The Parrot replied, "Your master has just bought me and brought me home with him." "You impudent bird," said the Cat, "how dare you, a newcomer, make a noise like that? Why, I was born here, and have lived here all my life, and yet, if I venture to mew, they throw things at me and chase me all over the place." "Look here, mistress," said the Parrot, "you just hold your tongue. My voice they delight in; but yours—yours is a perfect nuisance."

Philippians 2: 14
*Do all things without complaining and disputing...*

Proverbs 14: 30
*A sound heart is life to the body,*
*But envy is rottenness to the bones.*

# 195 :: The Partridge and The Fowler

A **Fowler** caught a **Partridge** in his nets, and was just about to wring its neck when it made a piteous appeal to him to spare its life and said, "Do not kill me, but let me live and I will repay you for your kindness by decoying other partridges into your nets." "No," said the Fowler, "I will not spare you. I was going to kill you anyhow, and after that treacherous speech you thoroughly deserve your fate."

# 196 :: The Peacock and Juno

The Peacock was greatly discontented because he had not a beautiful voice like the **nightingale**, and he went and complained to **Juno** about it. "The nightingale's song," said he, "is the envy of all the birds; but whenever I utter a sound I become a laughingstock." The goddess tried to console him by saying, "You have not, it is true, the power of song, but then you far excel all the rest in beauty: your neck flashes like the emerald and your splendid tail is a marvel of gorgeous colour." But the Peacock was not appeased. "What is the use," said he, "of being beautiful, with a voice like mine?" Then Juno replied, with a shade of sternness in her tones, "Fate has allotted to all their destined gifts: to yourself beauty, to the eagle strength, to the nightingale song, and so on to all the rest in their degree; but you alone are dissatisfied with your portion. Make, then, no more complaints. For, if your present wish were granted, you would quickly find cause for fresh discontent."

1 Timothy 6: 6
*Now godliness with contentment is great gain.*

# 197 :: The Peacock and The Crane

A Peacock taunted a **Crane** with the dullness of her plumage. "Look at my brilliant colours," said she, "and see how much finer they are than your poor feathers." "I am not denying," replied the Crane, "that yours are far gayer than mine; but when it comes to flying I can soar into the clouds, whereas you are confined to the earth like any dunghill **cock**."

# 198 :: The Peasant and The Apple-Tree

A Peasant had an Apple-tree growing in his garden, which bore no fruit, but merely served to provide a shelter from the heat for the sparrows and grasshoppers which sat and chirped in its branches. Disappointed at its barrenness he determined to cut it down, and went and fetched his axe for the purpose. But when the sparrows and the grasshoppers saw what he was about to do, they begged him to spare it, and said to him, "If you destroy the tree we shall have to seek shelter elsewhere, and you will no longer have our merry chirping to enliven your work in the garden." He, however, refused to listen to them, and set to work with a will to cut through the trunk. A few strokes showed that it was hollow inside and contained a swarm of bees and a large store of honey. Delighted with his find he threw down his axe, saying, "The old tree is worth keeping after all."

***Utility is most men's test of worth.***

Example: the Prophet Ezekiel is speaking of the outcast vine of Israel:

Ezekiel 15: 4b
*Is it useful for any work?*

## 199 :: The Pig and The Sheep

A Pig found his way into a meadow where a flock of Sheep were grazing. The shepherd caught him, and was proceeding to carry him off to the butcher's when he set up a loud squealing and struggled to get free. The Sheep rebuked him for making such a to-do, and said to him, "The shepherd catches us regularly and drags us off just like that, and we don't make any fuss." "No, I dare say not," replied the Pig, "but my case and yours are altogether different: he only wants you for wool, but he wants me for bacon."

## 200 :: The Ploughman and The Wolf

A **Ploughman** loosed his oxen from the plough, and led them away to the water to drink. While he was absent a half-starved Wolf appeared on the scene, and went up to the plough and began chewing the leather straps attached to the yoke. As he gnawed away desperately in the hope of satisfying his craving for food, he somehow got entangled in the harness, and, taking fright, struggled to get free, tugging at the traces as if he would drag the plough along with him. Just then the Ploughman came back, and seeing what was happening, he cried, "Ah, you old rascal, I wish you would give up thieving for good and take to honest work instead."

## 201 :: The Ploughman, The Ass, and The Ox

A **Ploughman** yoked his Ox and his **Ass** together, and set to work to plough his field. It was a poor makeshift of a team, but it was the best he could do, as he had but a single Ox. At the end of the day, when the beasts were loosed from the yoke, the Ass said to the Ox, "Well, we've had a hard day: which of us is to carry the master home?" The Ox looked surprised at the question. "Why," said he, "you, to be sure, as usual."

# 202 :: The Pomegranate, The Apple-Tree, and The Bramble

A Pomegranate and an Apple-tree were disputing about the quality of their fruits, and each claimed that its own was the better of the two. High words passed between them, and a violent quarrel was imminent, when a **Bramble** impudently poked its head out of a neighbouring hedge and said, "There, that's enough, my friends; don't let us quarrel."

# 203 :: The Prophet

A Prophet sat in the market-place and told the fortunes of all who cared to engage his services. Suddenly there came running up one who told him that his house had been broken into by thieves, and that they had made off with everything they could lay hands on. He was up in a moment, and rushed off, tearing his hair and calling down curses on the miscreants. The bystanders were much amused, and one of them said, "Our friend professes to know what is going to happen to others, but it seems he's not clever enough to perceive what's in store for himself."

1 John 4: 1
*Beloved, do not believe every spirit, but test the spirits, whether they are of God; because many false prophets have gone out into the world.*

## 204 :: The Quack Doctor

A certain man fell sick and took to his bed. He consulted a number of doctors from time to time, and they all, with one exception, told him that his life was in no immediate danger, but that his illness would probably last a considerable time. The one who took a different view of his case, who was also the last to be consulted, bade him prepare for the worst: "You have not twenty-four hours to live," said he, "and I fear I can do nothing." As it turned out, however, he was quite wrong; for at the end of a few days the sick man quitted his bed and took a walk abroad, looking, it is true, as pale as a ghost. In the course of his walk he met the Doctor who had prophesied his death. "Dear me," said the latter, "how do you do? You are fresh from the other world, no doubt. Pray, how are our departed friends getting on there?" "Most comfortably," replied the other, "for they have drunk the water of oblivion, and have forgotten all the troubles of life. By the way, just before I left, the authorities were making arrangements to prosecute all the doctors, because they won't let sick men die in the course of nature, but use their arts to keep them alive. They were going to charge you along with the rest, till I assured them that you were no doctor, but a mere impostor."

## 205 :: The Quack Frog

Once upon a time a Frog came forth from his home in the marshes and proclaimed to all the world that he was a learned physician, skilled in drugs and able to cure all diseases. Among the crowd was a Fox, who called out, "You a doctor! Why, how can you set up to heal others when you cannot even cure your own lame legs and blotched and wrinkled skin?"

***Physician, heal thyself.***

Matthew 7: 3
*And why do you look at the speck in your brother's eye, but do not consider the plank in your own eye?*

# 206 :: The Rich Man and The Tanner

A Rich Man took up his residence next door to a **Tanner**, and found the smell of the tan-yard so extremely unpleasant that he told him he must go. The Tanner delayed his departure, and the Rich Man had to speak to him several times about it; and every time the Tanner said he was making arrangements to move very shortly. This went on for some time, till at last the Rich Man got so used to the smell that he ceased to mind it, and troubled the Tanner with his objections no more.

# 207 :: The Rivers and The Sea

Once upon a time all the Rivers combined to protest against the action of the Sea in making their waters salt. "When we come to you," said they to the Sea, "we are sweet and drinkable: but when once we have mingled with you, our waters become as briny and unpalatable as your own." The Sea replied shortly, "Keep away from me and you'll remain sweet."

# 208 :: The Rogue and The Oracle

A **Rogue** laid a wager that he would prove the **Oracle at Delphi** to be untrustworthy by procuring from it a false reply to an inquiry by himself. So he went to the temple on the appointed day with a small bird in his hand, which he concealed under the folds of his cloak, and asked whether what he held in his hand were alive or dead. If the Oracle said "dead," he meant to produce the bird alive: if the reply was "alive," he intended to wring its neck and show it to be dead. But the Oracle was one too many for him, for the answer he got was this: "Stranger, whether the thing that you hold in your hand be alive or dead is a matter that depends entirely on your own will."

205 :: The Quack Frog page 149

# 209 :: The Rose and The Amaranth

A Rose and an **Amaranth** blossomed side by side in a garden, and the **Amaranth** said to her neighbour, "How I envy you your beauty and your sweet scent! No wonder you are such a universal favourite." But the Rose replied with a shade of sadness in her voice, "Ah, my dear friend, I bloom but for a time: my petals soon wither and fall, and then I die. But your flowers never fade, even if they are cut; for they are everlasting."

# 210 :: The Runaway Slave

A Slave, being discontented with his lot, ran away from his master. He was soon missed by the latter, who lost no time in mounting his horse and setting out in pursuit of the fugitive. He presently came up with him, and the Slave, in the hope of avoiding capture, slipped into a **treadmill** and hid himself there. "Aha," said his master, "that's the very place for you, my man!"

# 211 :: The Serpent and The Eagle

An Eagle swooped down upon a **Serpent** and seized it in his talons with the intention of carrying it off and devouring it. But the Serpent was too quick for him and had its coils round him in a moment; and then there ensued a life-and-death struggle between the two. A countryman, who was a witness of the encounter, came to the assistance of the Eagle, and succeeded in freeing him from the Serpent and enabling him to escape. In revenge the Serpent spat some of his poison into the man's drinking-horn. Heated with his exertions, the man was about to slake his thirst with a draught from the horn, when the Eagle knocked it out of his hand, and spilled its contents upon the ground.

***One good turn deserves another.***

Matthew 7: 12
*Therefore, whatever you want men to do to you, do also to them, for this is the Law and the Prophets.*

Luke 6: 38
*Give, and it will be given to you: good measure, pressed down, shaken together, and running over will be put into your bosom. For with the same measure that you use, it will be measured back to you.*

# 212 :: The Sheep and The Dog

Once upon a time the Sheep complained to the Shepherd about the difference in his treatment of themselves and his Dog. "Your conduct," said they, "is very strange and, we think, very unfair. We provide you with wool and lambs and milk and you give us nothing but grass, and even that we have to find for ourselves: but you get nothing at all from the Dog, and yet you feed him with tit-bits from your own table." Their remarks were overheard by the Dog, who spoke up at once and said, "Yes, and quite right, too: where would you be if it wasn't for me? Thieves would steal you! Wolves would eat you! Indeed, if I didn't keep constant watch over you, you would be too terrified even to graze!" The Sheep were obliged to acknowledge that he spoke the truth, and never again made a grievance of the regard in which he was held by his master.

# 213 :: The Sheep, The Wolf and The Stag

A **Stag** once asked a Sheep to lend him a measure of wheat, saying that his friend the Wolf would be his surety. The Sheep, however, was afraid that they meant to cheat her; so she excused herself, saying, "The Wolf is in the habit of seizing what he wants and running off with it without paying, and you, too, can run much faster than I. So how shall I be able to come up with either of you when the debt falls due?"

***Two blacks do not make a white.***

Example in which David tries to cover his sin with Bathsheba:

2 Samuel 11: 15
*And he wrote in the letter, saying, "Set Uriah in the forefront of the hottest battle, and retreat from him, that he may be struck down and die."*

# 214 :: The She-Goats and Their Beards

**Jupiter** granted beards to the She-goats at their own request, much to the disgust of the He-goats, who considered this to be an unwarrantable invasion of their rights and dignities. So they sent a deputation to him to protest against his action. He, however, advised them not to raise any objections. "What's in a tuft of hair?" said he. "Let them have it if they want it. They can never be a match for you in strength."

# 215 :: The Shepherd and The Wolf

A Shepherd found a Wolf's Cub straying in the pastures, and took him home and reared him along with his dogs. When the Cub grew to his full size, if ever a wolf stole a sheep from the flock, he used to join the dogs in hunting him down. It sometimes happened that the dogs failed to come up with the thief, and, abandoning the pursuit, returned home. The Wolf would on such occasions continue the chase by himself, and when he overtook the culprit, would stop and share the feast with him, and then return to the Shepherd. But if some time passed without a sheep being carried off by the wolves, he would steal one himself and share his plunder with the dogs. The Shepherd's suspicions were aroused, and one day he caught him in the act; and, fastening a rope round his neck, hung him on the nearest tree.

***What's bred in the bone is sure to come out in the flesh.***

2 Kings 15: 9
*And he did evil in the sight of the Lord, as his fathers had done; he did not depart from the sins of Jeroboam the son of Nebat, who had made Israel sin.*

# 216 :: The Shepherd's Boy and The Wolf

A Shepherd's Boy was tending his flock near a village, and thought it would be great fun to hoax the villagers by pretending that a Wolf was attacking the sheep: so he shouted out, "Wolf! wolf!" and when the people came running up he laughed at them for their pains. He did this more than once, and every time the villagers found they had been hoaxed, for there was no Wolf at all. At last a Wolf really did come, and the Boy cried, "Wolf! wolf!" as loud as he could: but the people were so used to hearing him call that they took no notice of his cries for help. And so the Wolf had it all his own way, and killed off sheep after sheep at his leisure.

***You cannot believe a liar even when he tells the truth.***

Zechariah 8: 16
*These are the things you shall do:*
*Speak each man the truth to his neighbor.*

# 217 :: The Shipwrecked Man and The Sea

A Shipwrecked Man cast up on the beach fell asleep after his struggle with the waves. When he woke up, he bitterly reproached the Sea for its treachery in enticing men with its smooth and smiling surface, and then, when they were well embarked, turning in fury upon them and sending both ship and sailors to destruction. The Sea arose in the form of a woman, and replied, "Lay not the blame on me, O sailor, but on the Winds. By nature I am as calm and safe as the land itself: but the Winds fall upon me with their gusts and gales, and lash me into a fury that is not natural to me."

# 218 :: The Sick Man and The Doctor

A Sick Man received a visit from his Doctor, who asked him how he was. "Fairly well, Doctor," said he, "but I find I sweat a great deal." "Ah," said the Doctor, "that's a good sign." On his next visit he asked the same question, and his patient replied, "I'm much as usual, but I've taken to having shivering fits, which leave me cold all over." "Ah," said the Doctor, "that's a good sign too." When he came the third time and inquired as before about his patient's health, the Sick Man said that he felt very feverish. "A very good sign," said the Doctor; "you are doing very nicely indeed." Afterwards a friend came to see the invalid, and on asking him how he did, received this reply: "My dear friend, I'm dying of good signs."

# 219 :: The Sick Stag

A **Stag** fell sick and lay in a clearing in the forest, too weak to move from the spot. When the news of his illness spread, a number of the other beasts came to inquire after his health, and they one and all nibbled a little of the grass that grew round the invalid till at last there was not a blade within his reach. In a few days he began to mend, but was still too feeble to get up and go in search of fodder; and thus he perished miserably of hunger owing to the thoughtlessness of his friends.

Matthew 25: 35
*...for I was hungry and you gave Me food; I was thirsty and you gave Me drink; I was a stranger and you took Me in...*

217 :: The Shipwrecked Man and The Sea page 156

# 220 :: The Slave and The Lion

A Slave ran away from his master, by whom he had been most cruelly treated, and, in order to avoid capture, betook himself into the desert. As he wandered about in search of food and shelter, he came to a cave, which he entered and found to be unoccupied. Really, however, it was a Lion's den, and almost immediately, to the horror of the wretched fugitive, the Lion himself appeared. The man gave himself up for lost: but, to his utter astonishment, the Lion, instead of springing upon him and devouring him, came and **fawned** upon him, at the same time whining and lifting up his paw. Observing it to be much swollen and inflamed, he examined it and found a large thorn embedded in the ball of the foot. He accordingly removed it and dressed the wound as well as he could: and in course of time it healed up completely. The Lion's gratitude was unbounded; he looked upon the man as his friend, and they shared the cave for some time together. A day came, however, when the Slave began to long for the society of his fellow-men, and he bade farewell to the Lion and returned to the town. Here he was presently recognised and carried off in chains to his former master, who resolved to make an example of him, and ordered that he should be thrown to the beasts at the next public spectacle in the theatre. On the fatal day the beasts were loosed into the arena, and among the rest a Lion of huge bulk and ferocious aspect; and then the wretched Slave was cast in among them. What was the amazement of the spectators, when the Lion after one glance bounded up to him and lay down at his feet with every expression of affection and delight! It was his old friend of the cave! The audience clamoured that the Slave's life should be spared: and the governor of the town, marvelling at such gratitude and fidelity in a beast, decreed that both should receive their liberty.

Hosea 10: 12
*Sow for yourselves righteousness;*
*Reap in mercy...*

Galatians 6: 9
*And let us not grow weary while doing good, for in due season we shall reap if we do not lose heart.*

# 221 :: The Snake and Jupiter

A Snake suffered a good deal from being constantly trodden upon by man and beast, owing partly to the length of his body and partly to his being unable to raise himself above the surface of the ground: so he went and complained to **Jupiter** about the risks to which he was exposed. But Jupiter had little sympathy for him. "I dare say," said he, "that if you had bitten the first that trod on you, the others would have taken more trouble to look where they put their feet."

# 222 :: The Soldier and His Horse

A Soldier gave his Horse a plentiful supply of oats in time of war, and tended him with the utmost care, for he wished him to be strong to endure the hardships of the field, and swift to bear his master, when need arose, out of the reach of danger. But when the war was over he employed him on all sorts of drudgery, bestowing but little attention upon him, and giving him, moreover, nothing but chaff to eat. The time came when war broke out again, and the Soldier saddled and bridled his Horse, and, having put on his heavy coat of mail, mounted him to ride off and take the field. But the poor half-starved beast sank down under his weight, and said to his rider, "You will have to go into battle on foot this time. Thanks to hard work and bad food, you have turned me from a Horse into an **ass**; and you cannot in a moment turn me back again into a Horse."

Proverbs 12: 10
*A righteous man regards the life of his animal,*
*But the tender mercies of the wicked are cruel.*

# 223 :: The Spendthrift and The Swallow

A **Spendthrift**, who had wasted his fortune, and had nothing left but the clothes in which he stood, saw a Swallow one fine day in early spring. Thinking that summer had come, and that he could now do without his coat, he went and sold it for what it would fetch. A change, however, took place in the weather, and there came a sharp frost which killed the unfortunate Swallow. When the Spendthrift saw its dead body he cried, "Miserable bird! Thanks to you I am perishing of cold myself."

***One swallow does not make summer.***

Proverbs 15: 21
*Folly is joy to him who is destitute ofdiscernment,*
*But a man of understanding walks uprightly.*

Ecclesiastes 3: 1
*To everything there is a season, A time for every purpose under heaven...*

# 224 :: The Stag and The Lion

A **Stag** was chased by the hounds, and took refuge in a cave, where he hoped to be safe from his pursuers. Unfortunately the cave contained a Lion, to whom he fell an easy prey. "Unhappy that I am," he cried, "I am saved from the power of the dogs only to fall into the clutches of a Lion."

***Out of the frying-pan into the fire.***

Proverbs 14: 12
*There is a way that seems right to a man,*
*But its end is the way of death.*

# 225 :: The Stag in the Ox-Stall

A **Stag**, chased from his lair by the hounds, took refuge in a farmyard, and, entering a stable where a number of Oxen were stalled, thrust himself under a pile of hay in a vacant stall, where he lay concealed, all but the tips of his horns. Presently one of the Oxen said to him, "What has induced you to come in here? Aren't you aware of the risk you are running of being captured by the herdsmen?" To which he replied, "Pray let me stay for the present. When night comes I shall easily escape under cover of the dark." In the course of the afternoon more than one of the farm-hands came in, to attend to the wants of the cattle, but not one of them noticed the presence of the Stag, who accordingly began to congratulate himself on his escape and to express his gratitude to the Oxen. "We wish you well," said the one who had spoken before, "but you are not out of danger yet. If the master comes, you will certainly be found out, for nothing ever escapes his keen eyes." Presently, sure enough, in he came, and made a great to-do about the way the Oxen were kept. "The beasts are starving," he cried; "here, give them more hay, and put plenty of litter under them." As he spoke, he seized an armful himself from the pile where the Stag lay concealed, and at once detected him. Calling his men, he had him seized at once and killed for the table.

# 226 :: The Stag and The Vine

A **Stag**, pursued by the huntsmen, concealed himself under cover of a thick Vine. They lost track of him and passed by his hiding-place without being aware that he was anywhere near. Supposing all danger to be over, he presently began to browse on the leaves of the Vine. The movement drew the attention of the returning huntsmen, and one of them, supposing some animal to be hidden there, shot an arrow at a venture into the foliage. The unlucky Stag was pierced to the heart, and, as he expired, he said, "I deserve my fate for my treachery in feeding upon the leaves of my protector."

***Ingratitude sometimes brings its own punishment.***

Deuteronomy 28: 47-48
*Because you did not serve the Lord your God with joyfulness of [mind and] heart [in gratitude] for the abundance of all [with which He had blessed you], Therefore you shall serve your enemies whom the Lord shall send against you, in hunger and thirst, in nakedness and in want of all things; and He will put a yoke of iron upon your neck until He has destroyed you. (AMP)*

# 227 :: The Stag at the Pool

A thirsty **Stag** went down to a pool to drink. As he bent over the surface he saw his own reflection in the water, and was struck with admiration for his fine spreading antlers, but at the same time he felt nothing but disgust for the weakness and slenderness of his legs. While he stood there looking at himself, he was seen and attacked by a Lion; but in the chase which ensued, he soon drew away from his pursuer, and kept his lead as long as the ground over which he ran was open and free of trees. But coming presently to a wood, he was caught by his antlers in the branches, and fell a victim to the teeth and claws of his enemy. "Woe is me!" he cried with his last breath; "I despised my legs, which might have saved my life: but I gloried in my horns, and they have proved my ruin."

***What is worth most is often valued least.***

Job 28: 12-13
*But where can wisdom be found?*
*And where is the place of understanding?*
*Man does not know its value,*
*Nor is it found in the land of the living.*

Example: King David's son, Absalom, had beautiful long hair that was his pride that ultimately led to his death.

2 Samuel 18: 9
*Then Absalom met the servants of David. Absalom rode on a mule. The mule went under the thick boughs of a great* ***terebinth tree****, and his head caught in the terebinth; so he was left hanging between heaven and earth. And the mule which was under him went on.*

# 228 :: The Stag with One Eye

A **Stag**, blind of one eye, was grazing close to the sea-shore and kept his sound eye turned towards the land, so as to be able to perceive the approach of the hounds, while the blind eye he turned towards the sea, never suspecting that any danger would threaten him from that quarter. As it fell out, however, some sailors, coasting along the shore, spied him and shot an arrow at him, by which he was mortally wounded. As he lay dying, he said to himself, "Wretch that I am! I bethought me of the dangers of the land, whence none assailed me: but I feared no peril from the sea, yet thence has come my ruin."

***Misfortune often assails us from an unexpected quarter.***

Job 12: 5
*In the thought of him who is at ease there is contempt for misfortune – but it is ready for those whose feet slip.*

# 229 :: The Swallow and The Crow

A Swallow was once boasting to a Crow about her birth. "I was once a princess," said she, "the daughter of a King of Athens, but my husband used me cruelly, and cut out my tongue for a slight fault. Then, to protect me from further injury, I was turned by **Juno** into a bird." "You chatter quite enough as it is," said the Crow. "What you would have been like if you hadn't lost your tongue, I can't think."

Proverbs 21: 9
*Better to dwell in a corner of a housetop,*
*Than in a house shared with a contentious woman.*

# 230 :: The Swan

The Swan is said to sing but once in its life—when it knows that it is about to die. A certain man, who had heard of the song of the Swan, one day saw one of these birds for sale in the market, and bought it and took it home with him. A few days later he had some friends to dinner, and produced the Swan, and bade it sing for their entertainment: but the Swan remained silent. In course of time, when it was growing old, it became aware of its approaching end and broke into a sweet, sad song. When its owner heard it, he said angrily, "If the creature only sings when it is about to die, what a fool I was that day I wanted to hear its song! I ought to have wrung its neck instead of merely inviting it to sing."

# 231 :: The Swollen Fox

A hungry Fox found in a hollow tree a quantity of bread and meat, which some shepherds had placed there against their return. Delighted with his find he slipped in through the narrow aperture and greedily devoured it all. But when he tried to get out again he found himself so swollen after his big meal that he could not squeeze through the hole, and fell to whining and groaning over his misfortune. Another Fox, happening to pass that way, came and asked him what the matter was; and, on learning the state of the case, said, "Well, my friend, I see nothing for it but for you to stay where you are till you shrink to your former size; you'll get out then easily enough."

# 232 :: The Thieves and The Cock

Some Thieves broke into a house, and found nothing worth taking except a **Cock**, which they seized and carried off with them. When they were preparing their supper, one of them caught up the Cock, and was about to wring his neck, when he cried out for mercy and said, "Pray do not kill me: you will find me a most useful bird, for I rouse honest men to their work in the morning by my crowing." But the Thief replied with some heat, "Yes, I know you do, making it still harder for us to get a livelihood. Into the pot you go!"

# 233 :: The Thief and The Innkeeper

A Thief hired a room at an inn, and stayed there some days on the look-out for something to steal. No opportunity, however, presented itself, till one day, when there was a festival to be celebrated, the Innkeeper appeared in a fine new coat and sat down before the door of the inn for an airing. The Thief no sooner set eyes upon the coat than he longed to get possession of it. There was no business doing, so he went and took a seat by the side of the Innkeeper, and began talking to him. They conversed together for some time, and then the Thief suddenly yawned and howled like a wolf. The Innkeeper asked him in some concern what ailed him. The Thief replied, "I will tell you about myself, sir, but first I must beg you to take charge of my clothes for me, for I intend to leave them with you. Why I have these fits of yawning I cannot tell: maybe they are sent as a punishment for my misdeeds; but, whatever the reason, the facts are that when I have yawned three times I become a ravening wolf and fly at men's throats." As he finished speaking he yawned a second time and howled again as before. The Innkeeper, believing every word he said, and terrified at the prospect of being confronted with a wolf, got up hastily and started to run indoors; but the Thief caught him by the coat and tried to stop him, crying, "Stay, sir, stay, and take charge of my clothes, or else I shall never see them again." As he spoke he opened his mouth and began to yawn for the third time. The Innkeeper, mad with the fear of being eaten by a wolf, slipped out of his coat, which remained in the other's hands, and bolted into the inn and locked the door behind him; and the Thief then quietly stole off with his spoil.

# 234 :: The Three Tradesmen

The citizens of a certain city were debating about the best material to use in the fortifications which were about to be erected for the greater security of the town. A Carpenter got up and advised the use of wood, which he said was readily procurable and easily worked. A Stone-mason objected to wood on the ground that it was so flammable, and recommended stones instead. Then a **Tanner** got on his legs and said, "In my opinion there's nothing like leather."

***Every man for himself.***

The intent of the fable is to reveal how each sees situations and solutions through the lense of his own knowledge and perceptions.

Job 34: 11
*For He repays man according to his work,*
*And makes man to find a reward according to his way.*

Proverbs 16: 9
*A man's heart plans his way, but the Lord directs his steps.*

# 235 :: The Tortoise and The Eagle

A Tortoise, discontented with his lowly life, and envious of the birds he saw disporting themselves in the air, begged an Eagle to teach him to fly. The Eagle protested that it was idle for him to try, as nature had not provided him with wings; but the Tortoise pressed him with entreaties and promises of treasure, insisting that it could only be a question of learning the craft of the air. So at length the Eagle consented to do the best he could for him, and picked him up in his talons. Soaring with him to a great height in the sky he then let him go, and the wretched Tortoise fell headlong and was dashed to pieces on a rock.

# 236 :: The Town Mouse and The Country Mouse

A Town Mouse and a Country Mouse were acquaintances, and the Country Mouse one day invited his friend to come and see him at his home in the fields. The Town Mouse came, and they sat down to a dinner of barleycorns and roots, the latter of which had a distinctly earthy flavour. The fare was not much to the taste of the guest, and presently he broke out with "My poor dear friend, you live here no better than the ants. Now, you should just see how I fare! My larder is a regular horn of plenty. You must come and stay with me, and I promise you you shall live on the fat of the land." So when he returned to town he took the Country Mouse with him, and showed him into a larder containing flour and oatmeal and figs and honey and dates. The Country Mouse had never seen anything like it, and sat down to enjoy the luxuries his friend provided: but before they had well begun, the door of the larder opened and some one came in. The two Mice scampered off and hid themselves in a narrow and exceedingly uncomfortable hole. Presently, when all was quiet, they ventured out again; but some one else came in, and off they scuttled again. This was too much for the visitor. "Good-bye," said he, "I'm off. You live in the lap of luxury, I can see, but you are surrounded by dangers; whereas at home I can enjoy my simple dinner of roots and corn in peace."

239 :: The Travellers and The Plane-Tree page 173

# 237 :: The Traveller and Fortune

A Traveller, exhausted with fatigue after a long journey, sank down at the very brink of a deep well and presently fell asleep. He was within an ace of falling in, when Dame **Fortune** appeared to him and touched him on the shoulder, cautioning him to move further away. "Wake up, good sir, I pray you," she said; "had you fallen into the well, the blame would have been thrown not on your own folly but on me, Fortune."

# 238 :: The Traveller and His Dog

A Traveller was about to start on a journey, and said to his Dog, who was stretching himself by the door, "Come, what are you yawning for? Hurry up and get ready: I mean you to go with me." But the Dog merely wagged his tail and said quietly, "I'm ready, master: it's you I'm waiting for."

Ecclesiastes 7: 8
*The end of a thing is better than its beginning;*
*The patient in spirit is better than the proud in spirit.*

# 239 :: The Travellers and The Plane-Tree

Two Travellers were walking along a bare and dusty road in the heat of a summer's day. Coming presently to a **Plane-tree**, they joyfully turned aside to shelter from the burning rays of the sun in the deep shade of its spreading branches. As they rested, looking up into the tree, one of them remarked to his companion, "What a useless tree the Plane is! It bears no fruit and is of no service to man at all." The Plane-tree interrupted him with indignation. "You ungrateful creature!" it cried: "you come and take shelter under me from the scorching sun, and then, in the very act of enjoying the cool shade of my foliage, you abuse me and call me good for nothing!"

***Many a service is met with ingratitude.***

Example: Jonah 4: 5-6
*So Jonah went out of the city and sat on the east side of the city. There he made himself a shelter and sat under it in the shade, till he might see what would become of the city. And the Lord God prepared a plant and made it come up over Jonah, that it might be shade for his head to deliver him from his misery. So Jonah was very grateful for the plant.*

Psalm 66: 8-9
*Bless our God, O peoples, give Him grateful thanks and make the voice of His praise be heard,*
*Who put and kept us among the living, and has not allowed our feet to slip. (AMP)*

240 :: The Trees and The Axe page 175

## 240 :: The Trees and The Axe

A Woodman went into the forest and begged of the Trees the favour of a handle for his Axe. The principal Trees at once agreed to so modest a request, and unhesitatingly gave him a young ash sapling, out of which he fashioned the handle he desired. No sooner had he done so than he set to work to fell the noblest Trees in the wood. When they saw the use to which he was putting their gift, they cried, "Alas! alas! We are undone, but we are ourselves to blame. The little we gave has cost us all: had we not sacrificed the rights of the ash, we might ourselves have stood for ages."

## 241 :: The Trumpeter Taken Prisoner

A Trumpeter marched into battle in the van of the army and put courage into his comrades by his warlike tunes. Being captured by the enemy, he begged for his life, and said, "Do not put me to death; I have killed no one: indeed, I have no weapons, but carry with me only my trumpet here." But his captors replied, "That is only the more reason why we should take your life; for, though you do not fight yourself, you stir up others to do so."

## 242 :: The Tunny-Fish and The Dolphin

A **Tunny-fish** was chased by a Dolphin and splashed through the water at a great rate, but the Dolphin gradually gained upon him, and was just about to seize him when the force of his flight carried the Tunny on to a sandbank. In the heat of the chase the Dolphin followed him, and there they both lay out of the water, gasping for dear life. When the Tunny saw that his enemy was doomed like himself, he said, "I don't mind having to die now: for I see that he who is the cause of my death is about to share the same fate."

# 243 :: The Two Bags

Every man carries Two Bags about with him, one in front and one behind, and both are packed full of faults. The Bag in front contains his neighbours' faults, the one behind his own. Hence it is that men do not see their own faults, but never fail to see those of others.

# 244 :: The Two Frogs

Two Frogs were neighbours. One lived in a marsh, where there was plenty of water, which frogs love: the other in a lane some distance away, where all the water to be had was that which lay in the ruts after rain. The Marsh Frog warned his friend and pressed him to come and live with him in the marsh, for he would find his quarters there far more comfortable and—what was still more important—more safe. But the other refused, saying that he could not bring himself to move from a place to which he had become accustomed. A few days afterwards a heavy waggon came down the lane, and he was crushed to death under the wheels.

# 245 :: The Two Pots

Two Pots, one of earthenware and the other of brass, were carried away down a river in flood. The Brazen Pot urged his companion to keep close by his side, and he would protect him. The other thanked him, but begged him not to come near him on any account: "For that," he said, "is just what I am most afraid of. One touch from you and I should be broken in pieces."

***Equals make the best friends.***

1 Samuel 18: 3
*Then Jonathan and David made a covenant, because he loved him as his own soul.*

2 Corinthians 6: 14
*Do not be unequally yoked together with unbelievers. For what fellowship has righteousness with lawlessness? And what communion has light with darkness?*

245 :: THE TWO POTS PAGE 176

# 246 :: The Two Soldiers and The Robber

Two Soldiers travelling together were set upon by a Robber. One of them ran away, but the other stood his ground, and laid about him so lustily with his sword that the Robber was fain to fly and leave him in peace. When the coast was clear the timid one ran back, and, flourishing his weapon, cried in a threatening voice, "Where is he? Let me get at him, and I'll soon let him know whom he's got to deal with." But the other replied, "You are a little late, my friend: I only wish you had backed me up just now, even if you had done no more than speak, for I should have been encouraged, believing your words to be true. As it is, calm yourself, and put up your sword: there is no further use for it. You may delude others into thinking you're as brave as a lion: but I know that, at the first sign of danger, you run away like a **hare**."

# 247 :: The Vain Jackdaw

**Jupiter** announced that he intended to appoint a king over the birds, and named a day on which they were to appear before his throne, when he would select the most beautiful of them all to be their ruler. Wishing to look their best on the occasion they repaired to the banks of a stream, where they busied themselves in washing and preening their feathers. The **Jackdaw** was there along with the rest, and realised that, with his ugly plumage, he would have no chance of being chosen as he was: so he waited till they were all gone, and then picked up the most gaudy of the feathers they had dropped, and fastened them about his own body, with the result that he looked gayer than any of them. When the appointed day came, the birds assembled before Jupiter's throne; and, after passing them in review, he was about to make the Jackdaw king, when all the rest set upon the king-elect, stripped him of his borrowed plumes, and exposed him for the Jackdaw that he was.

# 248 :: The Viper and The File

A **Viper** entered a carpenter's shop, and went from one to another of the tools, begging for something to eat. Among the rest, he addressed himself to the **File**, and asked for the favour of a meal. The File replied in a tone of pitying contempt, "What a simpleton you must be if you imagine you will get anything from me, who invariably take from every one and never give anything in return."

***The covetous are poor givers.***

Example regarding Israel's leaders: Isaiah 56: 11a
*Yes, they are greedy dogs*
*Which never have enough.*

2 Corinthians 9: 7
*So let each one give as he purposes in his heart, not grudgingly or of necessity; for God loves a cheerful giver.*

# 249 :: The Walnut-Tree

A Walnut-tree, which grew by the roadside, bore every year a plentiful crop of nuts. Every one who passed by pelted its branches with sticks and stones, in order to bring down the fruit, and the tree suffered severely. "It is hard," it cried, "that the very persons who enjoy my fruit should thus reward me with insults and blows."

## 250 :: The Wasp and The Snake

A Wasp settled on the head of a Snake, and not only stung him several times, but clung obstinately to the head of his victim. Maddened with pain the Snake tried every means he could think of to get rid of the creature, but without success. At last he became desperate, and crying, "Kill you I will, even at the cost of my own life," he laid his head with the Wasp on it under the wheel of a passing waggon, and they both perished together.

## 251 :: The Weasel and The Man

A Man once caught a Weasel, which was always sneaking about the house, and was just going to drown it in a tub of water, when it begged hard for its life, and said to him, "Surely you haven't the heart to put me to death? Think how useful I have been in clearing your house of the mice and lizards which used to infest it, and show your gratitude by sparing my life." "You have not been altogether useless, I grant you," said the Man: "but who killed the fowls? Who stole the meat? No, no! You do much more harm than good, and die you shall."

## 252 :: The Wild Boar and The Fox

A Wild **Boar** was engaged in whetting his tusks upon the trunk of a tree in the forest when a Fox came by and, seeing what he was at, said to him, "Why are you doing that, pray? The huntsmen are not out to-day, and there are no other dangers at hand that I can see." "True, my friend," replied the Boar, "but the instant my life is in danger I shall need to use my tusks. There'll be no time to sharpen them then."

## 253 :: The Wily Lion

A Lion watched a fat Bull feeding in a meadow, and his mouth watered when he thought of the royal feast he would make, but he did not dare to attack him, for he was afraid of his sharp horns. Hunger, however, presently compelled him to do something: and as the use of force did not promise success, he determined to resort to artifice. Going up to the Bull in friendly fashion, he said to him, "I cannot help saying how much I admire your magnificent figure. What a fine head! What powerful shoulders and thighs! But, my dear friend, what in the world makes you wear those ugly horns? You must find them as awkward as they are unsightly. Believe me, you would do much better without them." The Bull was foolish enough to be persuaded by this flattery to have his horns cut off; and, having now lost his only means of defence, fell an easy prey to the Lion.

## 254 :: The Witch

A Witch professed to be able to avert the anger of the gods by means of charms, of which she alone possessed the secret; and she drove a brisk trade, and made a fat livelihood out of it. But certain persons accused her of black magic and carried her before the judges, and demanded that she should be put to death for dealings with the Devil. She was found guilty and condemned to death: and one of the judges said to her as she was leaving the dock, "You say you can avert the anger of the gods. How comes it, then, that you have failed to disarm the enmity of men?"

## 255 :: The Wolf and His Shadow

A Wolf, who was roaming about on the plain when the sun was getting low in the sky, was much impressed by the size of his shadow, and said to himself, "I had no idea I was so big. Fancy my being afraid of a lion! Why, I, not he, ought to be King of the beasts"; and, heedless of danger, he strutted about as if there could be no doubt at all about it. Just then a lion sprang upon him and began to devour him. "Alas," he cried, "had I not lost sight of the facts, I shouldn't have been ruined by my fancies."

## 256 :: The Wolf and The Boy

A Wolf, who had just enjoyed a good meal and was in a playful mood, caught sight of a Boy lying flat upon the ground, and, realising that he was trying to hide, and that it was fear of himself that made him do this, he went up to him and said, "Aha, I've found you, you see; but if you can say three things to me, the truth of which cannot be disputed, I will spare your life." The Boy plucked up courage and thought for a moment, and then he said, "First, it is a pity you saw me; secondly, I was a fool to let myself be seen; and thirdly, we all hate wolves because they are always making unprovoked attacks upon our flocks." The Wolf replied, "Well, what you say is true enough from your point of view; so you may go."

## 257 :: The Wolf and The Crane

A Wolf once got a bone stuck in his throat. So he went to a **Crane** and begged her to put her long bill down his throat and pull it out. "I'll make it worth your while," he added. The Crane did as she was asked, and got the bone out quite easily. The Wolf thanked her warmly, and was just turning away, when she cried, "What about that fee of mine?" "Well, what about it?" snapped the Wolf, baring his teeth as he spoke; "you can go about boasting that you once put your head into a Wolf's mouth and didn't get it bitten off. What more do you want?"

257 :: The Wolf and The Crane Page 183

# 258 :: The Wolf and The Goat

A Wolf caught sight of a Goat browsing above him on the scanty herbage that grew on the top of a steep rock; and being unable to get at her, tried to induce her to come lower down. "You are risking your life up there, madam, indeed you are," he called out: "pray take my advice and come down here, where you will find plenty of better food." The Goat turned a knowing eye upon him. "It's little you care whether I get good grass or bad," said she: "what you want is to eat me."

258 :: The Wolf and The Goat page 184

# 259 :: The Wolf and The Horse

A Wolf on his rambles came to a field of oats, but, not being able to eat them, he was passing on his way when a Horse came along. "Look," said the Wolf, "here's a fine field of oats. For your sake I have left it untouched, and I shall greatly enjoy the sound of your teeth munching the ripe grain." But the Horse replied, "If wolves could eat oats, my fine friend, you would hardly have indulged your ears at the cost of your belly."

***There is no virtue in giving to others what is useless to oneself.***

Example: Luke 11: 42
*But woe to you Pharisees! For you tithe mint and rue and all manner of herbs, and pass by justice and the love of God. These you ought to have done, without leaving the others undone.*

James 1: 27
*Pure and undefiled religion before God and the Father is this: to visit orphans and widows in their trouble, and to keep oneself unspotted from the world.*

# 260 :: The Wolf and The Lamb

A Wolf came upon a Lamb straying from the flock, and felt some compunction about taking the life of so helpless a creature without some plausible excuse; so he cast about for a grievance and said at last, "Last year, sirrah, you grossly insulted me." "That is impossible, sir," bleated the Lamb, "for I wasn't born then." "Well," retorted the Wolf, "you feed in my pastures." "That cannot be," replied the Lamb, "for I have never yet tasted grass." "You drink from my spring, then," continued the Wolf. "Indeed, sir," said the poor Lamb, "I have never yet drunk anything but my mother's milk." "Well, anyhow," said the Wolf, "I'm not going without my dinner": and he sprang upon the Lamb and devoured it without more ado.

***A wicked man will always find an excuse for his evil doing.***

Psalm 7: 14
*Behold, the wicked brings forth iniquity;*
*Yes, he conceives trouble and brings forth falsehood.*

Psalm 32: 2
*Blessed is the man to whom the Lord does not impute iniquity,*
*And in whose spirit there is no deceit.*

# 261 :: The Wolf and The Lion

A Wolf stole a lamb from the flock, and was carrying it off to devour it at his leisure when he met a Lion, who took his prey away from him and walked off with it. He dared not resist, but when the Lion had gone some distance he said, "It is most unjust of you to take what's mine away from me like that." The Lion laughed and called out in reply, "It was justly yours, no doubt! The gift of a friend, perhaps, eh?"

## 262 :: The Wolf and The Sheep

A Wolf was worried and badly bitten by dogs, and lay a long time for dead. By and by he began to revive, and, feeling very hungry, called out to a passing Sheep and said, "Would you kindly bring me some water from the stream close by? I can manage about meat, if only I could get something to drink." But this Sheep was no fool. "I can quite understand," said he, "that if I brought you the water, you would have no difficulty about the meat. Good-morning."

## 263 :: The Wolf and The Shepherd

A Wolf hung about near a flock of sheep for a long time, but made no attempt to molest them. The Shepherd at first kept a sharp eye on him, for he naturally thought he meant mischief: but as time went by and the Wolf showed no inclination to meddle with the flock, he began to look upon him more as a protector than as an enemy: and when one day some errand took him to the city, he felt no uneasiness at leaving the Wolf with the sheep. But as soon as his back was turned the Wolf attacked them and killed the greater number. When the Shepherd returned and saw the havoc he had wrought, he cried, "It serves me right for trusting my flock to a Wolf."

## 264 :: The Wolf in Sheep's Clothing

A Wolf resolved to disguise himself in order that he might prey upon a flock of sheep without fear of detection. So he clothed himself in a sheepskin, and slipped among the sheep when they were out at pasture. He completely deceived the shepherd, and when the flock was penned for the night he was shut in with the rest. But that very night as it happened, the shepherd, requiring a supply of mutton for the table, laid hands on the Wolf in mistake for a Sheep, and killed him with his knife on the spot.

# 265 :: The Wolf, The Fox, and The Ape

A Wolf charged a Fox with theft, which he denied, and the case was brought before an Ape to be tried. When he had heard the evidence on both sides, the Ape gave judgment as follows: "I do not think," he said, "that you, O Wolf, ever lost what you claim; but all the same I believe that you, Fox, are guilty of the theft, in spite of all your denials."

***The dishonest get no credit, even if they act honestly.***

Proverbs 26: 24-25
*He who hates, disguises it with his lips,*
*And lays up deceit within himself;*
*When he speaks kindly, do not believe him,*
*For there are seven abominations in his heart...*

# 266 :: The Wolf, The Mother, and Her Child

A hungry Wolf was prowling about in search of food. By and by, attracted by the cries of a Child, he came to a cottage. As he crouched beneath the window, he heard the Mother say to the Child, "Stop crying, do! or I'll throw you to the Wolf." Thinking she really meant what she said, he waited there a long time in the expectation of satisfying his hunger. In the evening he heard the Mother fondling her Child and saying, "If the naughty Wolf comes, he shan't get my little one: Daddy will kill him." The Wolf got up in much disgust and walked away: "As for the people in that house," said he to himself, "you can't believe a word they say."

# 267 :: The Wolves and The Dogs

Once upon a time the Wolves said to the Dogs, "Why should we continue to be enemies any longer? You are very like us in most ways: the main difference between us is one of training only. We live a life of freedom; but you are enslaved to mankind, who beat you, and put heavy collars round your necks, and compel you to keep watch over their flocks and herds for them, and, to crown all, they give you nothing but bones to eat. Don't put up with it any longer, but hand over the flocks to us, and we will all live on the fat of the land and feast together." The Dogs allowed themselves to be persuaded by these words, and accompanied the Wolves into their den. But no sooner were they well inside than the Wolves set upon them and tore them to pieces.

***Traitors richly deserve their fate.***

Example: Esther 7:10
*So they hanged Haman on the gallows that he had prepared for Mordecai.*

(Read the Book of Esther for the full story of Haman's treachery.)

Example: Mark 14: 10
*Then Judas Iscariot, one of the twelve, went to the chief priests to betray Him to them.*

And Judas' fate: Matthew 27: 3-9.

# 268 :: The Wolves, The Sheep, and The Ram

The Wolves sent a deputation to the Sheep with proposals for a lasting peace between them, on condition of their giving up the sheep-dogs to instant death. The foolish Sheep agreed to the terms; but an old Ram, whose years had brought him wisdom, interfered and said, "How can we expect to live at peace with you? Why, even with the dogs at hand to protect us, we are never secure from your murderous attacks!"

# 269 :: The Woman and The Farmer

A Woman, who had lately lost her husband, used to go every day to his grave and lament her loss. A Farmer, who was engaged in ploughing not far from the spot, set eyes upon the Woman and desired to have her for his wife: so he left his plough and came and sat by her side, and began to shed tears himself. She asked him why he wept; and he replied, "I have lately lost my wife, who was very dear to me, and tears ease my grief." "And I," said she, "have lost my husband." And so for a while they mourned in silence. Then he said, "Since you and I are in like case, shall we not do well to marry and live together? I shall take the place of your dead husband, and you, that of my dead wife." The Woman consented to the plan, which indeed seemed reasonable enough: and they dried their tears. Meanwhile, a thief had come and stolen the oxen which the Farmer had left with his plough. On discovering the theft, he beat his breast and loudly bewailed his loss. When the Woman heard his cries, she came and said, "Why, are you weeping still?" To which he replied, "Yes, and I mean it this time."

# 270 :: Venus and The Cat

A Cat fell in love with a handsome young man, and begged the goddess **Venus** to change her into a woman. Venus was very gracious about it, and changed her at once into a beautiful maiden, whom the young man fell in love with at first sight and shortly afterwards married. One day Venus thought she would like to see whether the Cat had changed her habits as well as her form; so she let a mouse run loose in the room where they were. Forgetting everything, the young woman had no sooner seen the mouse than up she jumped and was after it like a shot: at which the goddess was so disgusted that she changed her back again into a Cat.

270 :: Venus and The Cat page 192

# For Further Study and Enjoyment

We include the following suggestions for educators, students and parents who would like to learn more from Aesop's Fables.

**Finding a Moral**

Not every fable in this edition has a moral. In fact, the inclusion of morals was not begun until the sixteenth century. Early hearers of the fables did not have the advantage of the moral to reinforce meaning. Take a fable which has no moral and create your own. If you are having difficulty, ask yourself what human trait does the character have? Alternately, retell the fable in your own words. Often a moral will suggest itself.

**Noting Scripture References**

Many more Scriptures could have been added to the ones already given if space allowed. Do you have additional Scriptures you would like to add? If you prefer not to note them in your book, we suggest you take 8 1/2 x 11 sheets of paper, fold them in half and staple on the fold. Then you have a small booklet to tuck in the back for your notes.

**Studying Scripture Along With the Fables**

To get help in finding additional Scripture use a Strong's Concordance or a Nave's Topical Index. Both of these can be found in print or online. To find an online version, simply type the title into a search box and include the word "online" at the end. You will have many sites from which to choose.

**Narrating fables**

Narration is telling back in one's own words what has been read aloud. It is a natural way to demonstrate and organize learning. Use one fable a day for several weeks; read it aloud once to your child and ask him to tell it back. You will likely be amazed at the colorful interpretations that spring from young minds. If you are new to the concept of narration we invite you to read "Successful Narration" at

our website Living Books Curriculum:
<www.livingbookscurriculum.com/successfulnarration.htm>.

**Creative Writing with Fables**

Have older children rewrite a fable in their own words. Because the story is already there, rewriting in one's own words builds confidence in the use of language. Encourage creativity.

**Using Fables in Your Devotions**

Using fables for devotions may sound like a strange idea but, as we studied to find Scriptures for the *Living Books Press Aesop's Fables* we found ourselves often meditating on God's Word. Sometimes the words of Scriptures, even modern language ones, leave us unclear. With a fable set alongside Scripture we found it easier to understand once obscure passages. We pray you will too.

**Illustrating Fables**

For students with an artistic inclination another way to "think on" the fables is to illustrate them. Make a book of illustrations and narrations of the fables. Art students at the University of Massachusetts were asked to illustrate a fable as part of their work. For inspiration, view the results at <www.umass.edu/aesop/index.php>.

**Imagine**

People usually regret when their actions harm others. Fables include characters that have behaved badly. Choose a fable character and have him write/compose an apology letter to the character he has treated poorly (i.e. hare teasing tortoise prior to race; city mouse critical of country mouse's home; lion laughing at mouse being able to help him).

**Writing Applications or Reflections for the Fables**

Other editions of Aesop's Fables include what are termed "Applications" or "Reflections". Still others have written "Mottos" which are rhyming couplets that underscore some meaning or purpose in the fable. Listed under "books" below are editions of Aesop's Fables that provide one or more of these additions. Enjoy reading through them. Most were written in an earlier time by Christians.

Additionally, write your own application or reflection for a fable. Collect several retellings of fables and the applications/reflections in a book and you have a real treasure.

**Books**

Claxton, William, (1484) *The history and fables of Aesop.* Modern reprint edited by Robert T. Lenaghan (Harvard University Press: Cambridge, 1967).

Croxall, Samuel, *The Fables of Aesop, with new applications, morals, etc. by Rev. Ceo. Flyer Townsend.* Now out of print, it can be found as an e-text online at <www.google.com/books>.

Handford, S. A., *Fables of Aesop.* (Penguin: New York, 1954)

Jacobs, Joseph, *The Fables of Aesop: Selected, Told Anew, and Their History Traced.* (A later version of Claxton's work by a renowned folklorist. Now out of print, it can be found as an e-text online at <www.gutenberg.org>.)

L'Estrange, Sir Roger. *Aesop's Fables.* (1692) Dover Books edition available.

Townsend, George Fyler. *Three-Hundred Aesop's Fables.* Now out of print, it can be found as an e-text online at <www.google.com/books>.

Winter, Milo. *The Aesop for Children with pictures by Milo Winter.* Stunning illustrations by early twentieth-century illustrator. Now out of print, it can be found as an e-text online at <www.gutenberg.org>.

**Web sites**

Aesopica: Aesop's Fables in English, Latin and Greek: <www.mythfolklore.net/aesopica/index.htm>.
(Very comprehensive, a treasure for the Aesop scholar.)

Aesop's Fables Online collection: <www.aesopfables.com>.
(Includes many fables, not all Aesop's.)

Audio versions of the Aesop's Fables:
<http://librivox.org/newcatalog>.
Type "Aesop" in search.

Carlson Fable Collection at Creighton University:
<http://aesop.creighton.edu/jcupub>.

# Word Glossary

Definitions compiled by
Eli J. Litzelman
Homeschool student, Jackson, Wyoming.

**Glossary words are bold text.**

**Amaranth:** (Amarantus) A coarse annual herb; the root Greek word (amarantos) means unfading. The word has also come to denote a flower that never fades.

**Apiary:** A place where bees are kept.

**Ass:** A donkey.

**Axletrees:** Any straight, strong tree, used to make wagon axles (**axle**: the shaft on which the wheels are placed.)

**Balzac:** Honoré de Balzac (1799-1850). Nineteenth-century French novelist and playwright.

**Blackamoor:** A dark-skinned person.

**Blacksmith:** A worker in metals who forges iron. (From a distinction between black metal, iron, and white metal, tin.)

**Boar:** A male pig.

**Babrius:** Greek writer of fables.

**Bramble:** A prickly shrub.

**Charcoal-burner:** (An occupation.) A man who makes charcoal.

**Charger:** Spirited horse; often used as a war horse.

**Chesterton, G.K.:** (1874-1963) An influential English writer of the early twentieth century. His prolific and diverse output included journalism, poetry, biography, Christian apologetics, fantasy, and detective fiction.

**Cobbler:** (An occupation.) A person who makes shoes.

**Cock:** Rooster.

**Crane** (bird): A large, long-legged bird.

**Croesus:** King of Lydia from 560 BC to 561 BC. Croesus was renowned for his wealth.

**Crown:** An old British silver coin worth 5 shillings (half-crown: British coin worth 2 shillings and 6 pence; shilling = 12 pence; pence = 1/100th of a pound); used as legal tender until 1970.

**Demeter:** In Greek religion and mythology, goddess of harvest and fertility; daughter of Kronos and Rhea. She was the mother of Persephone by Zeus. When Pluto abducted Persephone, Demeter grieved so inconsolably that the earth became barren through her neglect. Searching for her daughter, she wandered to Eleusis, where the Eleusinian Mysteries were inaugurated in her honor. She revealed to Triptolemus, an Eleusinian, the art of growing and using corn. The Thesmophoria, a fertility festival held in her honor at Athens, was attended only by women. The Romans identified her with Ceres.

**Dionysia:** Ancient Greek festivals held seasonally, chiefly at Athens, in honor of Dionysus, especially those held in the fall and connected with the development of early Greek drama.

**Draught-mule:** A mule adapted for drawing heavy loads. U.S. spelling "draft".

**Dunder-headed:** Thick-headed; stupid.

**Epigram:** Any witty, ingenious, or pointed saying expressed briefly and to the point.

**Ethiopian:** A person from Ethiopia, a country in Africa situated in the eastern part in what is called "The Horn of Africa".

**Fable:** A short tale to teach a moral lesson, often with animals or inanimate objects.

**Faggot:** A bundle of twigs, sticks, or branches.

**Fawn:** A young deer.

**Fawned:** Tried to gain favor by weakly submitting or groveling.

**Filberts:** A kind of nut. Middle English, from Old French (nois de) filbert, (nut of) Philbert, after Saint Philibert (died 684), whose feast day in late August coincides with the ripening of the nut.

**File:** A file (or hand-file) is a hand tool used to shape material by cutting. A file typically takes the form of a hardened steel bar, mostly covered with a series of sharp, parallel ridges or teeth.

**Form:** A lair; a den or resting place of a wild animal.

**Fortune** (A god): A mythical being of Greek mythology. Named Tykhe, she was credited as being the guide and conductor of the affairs of the world.

**Fowler:** (An occupation.) A hunter of birds.

**Fuller:** (An occupation.) A person who fulls cloth. Fulling is the process of washing the oils from the wool to prepare it for weaving.

**Gnat:** Any of certain small flies.

**Goatherd:** (An occupation.) A person who tends goats.

**Goddess of the Earth** (Greek mythology): Guardian of the earth. In Greek mythology her name was Demeter.

**Grimm Tales:** Referring to *Grimm's Fairy Tales*, a collection of German and French fairy tales, first published in 1812 by Jacob and Wilhelm Grimm, the "Brothers Grimm".

**Groom:** (An occupation.) A person responsible for the feeding and care of horses..

**Hare:** Any rodentlike mammal of the genus *Lepus*, of the family *Leporidae*, having long ears, a divided upper lip, and long hind limbs adapted for leaping; looks similar to a rabbit.

**Hedgehog:** An Old World, insect-eating mammal of the genus *Erinaceus, esp. E. europaeus,* having spiny hairs on the back and sides.

**Heifer:** A young cow over one year old that has not produced a calf.

**Hercules:** Also called Heracles and Alcides. From Greek mythology; a celebrated hero, the son of Zeus and Alcmene, possessing exceptional strength.

**Herodotus of Halcarnassus** (484 BC-425 BC): A Greek historian from Ionia who is regarded as the "father of history". He is known for writing "The Histories", a record of his inquiries into the origins of the Greco-Persian Wars which, a period of time and events that would otherwise have been poorly documented.

**Hind:** A deer. Usually refers to the red deer, the largest species of deer in the world, which inhabits Europe and Asia.

**Hymettus:** A mountain in south eastern Greece, near Athens. 3370 ft. (1027 m).

**Iniquity:** Injustice; unrighteousness; (an act of) wickedness; absence of moral or spiritual values.

**Jackdaw:** A glossy black, European bird, *Corvus monedula*, of the crow family, that nests in towers, ruins, etc. Looks very similar to an American Grackle.

**Juno:** A goddess. The ancient Roman queen of heaven, a daughter of Saturn and the wife and sister of Jupiter: the protector of women and marriage.

**Jupiter:** Also called Jove, the supreme deity of the ancient Romans: the god of the heavens and of weather.

**Kite** (bird): Any of several small birds of the hawk family *Accipitridae* that have long, pointed wings, feed on insects, carrion, reptiles, rodents, and birds, and are noted for their graceful, gliding flight.

**La Fontaine:** French writer who collected the stories of Aesop and others in his *Fables* (1668-1694).

**Larder:** A room or place where food is kept; pantry.

**Mabinogian:** The Mabinogion is a collection of prose stories from medieval Welsh manuscripts. They are partly based on early medieval historical events, but almost certainly hark back to older Iron Age traditions.

**Malory:** Referring to Sir Thomas Malory, the author of the most famous and influential prose version of the legends of King Arthur, called "Le Morte d'Arthur".

**Mappe:** The Anglo-Saxon word for "map".

**Mercury:** The ancient Roman god who served as messenger of the gods and was also the god of commerce, thievery, eloquence, and science, identified with the Greek god Hermes.

**Milkmaid:** (An occupation.) A woman who milks cows or is employed in a dairy; dairymaid.

**Miller:** (An occupation.) A person who owns or operates a grist mill in which grain is ground into flour.

**Millstone:** Either of a pair of circular stones between which grain or another substance is ground.

**Minerva:** The ancient Roman goddess of wisdom and the arts, identified with the Greek goddess Athena.

**Miser:** A person who lives in wretched circumstances in order to save and hoard money.

**Nettles:** Any of various hairy, stinging, or prickly plants.

**Nightingale:** Any of several small Old World migratory birds of the thrush family, esp. *Luscinia megarhynchos*, of Europe, noted for the melodious song of the male, given chiefly at night during the breeding season.

**Olympus:** A mountain in northeastern Greece, on the boundary between Thessaly and Macedonia: mythical abode of the greater Grecian gods. 9730 ft. (2966 m).

**Oracle:** An utterance, often ambiguous or obscure, given by a priest or priestess at a shrine as the response of a god to an inquiry.

**Oracle at Delphi:** Dating back to 1400 BC, the Oracle at Delphi was the most important shrine in all Greece, and in theory all Greeks respected its independence. Built around a sacred spring, Delphi was considered to be the omphalos—the center (literally navel) of the world.

**Panathenea:** A festival in honor of the goddess Athena, celebrated yearly in ancient Athens, with each fourth year reserved for greater pomp, marked by contests, as in athletics and music, and highlighted by a solemn procession to the Acropolis bearing a **peplos** embroidered for the goddess.

**Pannier:** Basket or pouch; particularly one of a pair to be slung across the shoulders or across the back of a beast.

**Partridge:** Any of several Old World game birds of the subfamily *Perdicinae,* esp. *Perdix perdix*. These are heavy-bodied birds in the same family as pheasant and grouse.

**Peplos:** A loose-fitting outer garment worn, draped in folds, by women in ancient Greece

**Perjury:** Lying under oath; the act of swearing something is true when one knows it is false.

**Perrault, Charles** (1628-1703): A French author who laid the foundations for the fairy tale as a literary genre.

**Phrygia:** A kingdom in the west central part of what is now Turkey. It eventually became a part of the Roman Empire.

**Piraeus:** A seaport in southeastern Greece; the port of Athens.

**Plane-tree:** Any tree of the genus *Platanus,* esp. *P. occidentalis*, the buttonwood or sycamore of North America, having palmately lobed leaves and bark that sheds.

**Ploughman:** An occupation. A man who plows. The spelling is British. U.S. spelling "plowman".

**Prevarication:** A lie.

**Quack:** A dishonest person who pretends to be a doctor.

**Reynard:** As in *Reynard the Fox*; a trickster figure whose tale is told in a number of tales from Medieval Europe.

**Rogue:** A dishonest, knavish person; scoundrel.

**Rook:** A European crow, *Corvus frugilegus*, noted for its gregarious habits.

**Rhodes:** An island situated west off the Turkish shore, situated between the Greek mainland and the island of Cyprus. The Colossus of Rhodes was one of the Seven Wonders of the World.

**Rustic:** A country person; possibly a goat-herd

**Satyr:** From classical mythology. One of a class of woodland deities, attendant on Bacchus, represented as part human, part horse, and sometimes part goat and noted for being loud and bawdy.

**Saul:** King of Israel before David. He was envious of David's favor with God and man.

**Serpent:** A snake.

**Solomon:** Tenth-century B.C. king of Israel (son of David), considered the wisest man who ever lived.

**Sow:** A female pig.

**Spendthrift:** A person who spends possessions or money extravagantly or wastefully.

**Sprat:** A fish; a species of herring, *Clupea sprattus*, of the eastern North Atlantic.

**Stag:** An adult male deer.

**Starling:** A chunky, medium-sized European perching bird, *Sturnus vulgaris*, of iridescent black plumage with seasonal speckles, that nests in colonies. Often considered a pest.

**Stork:** Any of several wading birds of the family *Ciconiidae*, having long legs and a long neck and bill.

**Tanner:** An occupation. One who converts a hide into leather, especially by soaking or steeping in a bath prepared from tanbark, or synthetically.

**Terebinth tree:** A small Medeterranean tree of the cashew family; yeilds Chian turpentine.

**Theban:** A person who lives in **Thebes**.

**Thebes:** An ancient city in Upper Egypt, on the Nile, whose ruins are located in the modern towns of Karnak and Luxor: a former capital of Egypt.

**Theseus:** A legendary king of Athens famous for many exploits in time of war. His most famous was slaying the Minotaur.

**Tow:** A tuft of wool for spinning, or the coarse and broken part of flax or hemp.

**Treadmill:** A non-motorized apparatus for producing rotary motion by the weight of people or animals, treading on a succession of moving steps or a belt that forms a kind of continuous path, as around the periphery of a pair of horizontal cylinders; treadmills were often used to grind grain. The word also is used to describe any monotonous, wearisome routine or task in which there is little or no satisfactory progress.

**Tunny-fish:** A tuna fish.

**Uncle Remus:** A fictional character, the title character and fictional narrator of a collection of black folktales adapted and compiled by Joel Chandler Harris, published in book form in 1881.

**Venus:** An ancient Italian goddess of gardens and spring, identified by the Romans with Aphrodite as the goddess of love and beauty.

**Viper:** Any of several venomous Old World snakes of the genus *Vipera*, esp. *V. berus*, a small snake common in northern Eurasia.

**Vixen:** A female fox.

# Alphabetical List of Morals

*A hypocrite deceives no one but himself.*
The Bear and The Fox, p. 20

*A man is known by the company he keeps.*
The Ass and His Purchaser, p. 7

*A villain may disguise himself, but he will not deceive the wise.*
The Cat and The Birds, p. 33

*Advantages that are dearly bought are doubtful blessings.*
The Pack-Ass and the Wild Ass, p. 143

*All men are more concerned to recover what they lose than to acquire what they lack.*
The Bat, The Bramble, and The Seagull, p. 19

*A wicked man will always find an excuse for his evil doing.*
The Wolf and The Lamb, p. 187

*Be content with your lot.*
The Crab and The Fox, p. 40

*Be shy of favours bestowed at the expense of others.*
The Dog and The Cook, p. 44

*Betray a friend, and you'll often find you have ruined yourself.*
The Ass, The Fox, and The Lion, p. 14

*Better poverty without care than wealth with its many obligations.*
The Fir-Tree and The Bramble, p. 62

*Better servitude with safety than freedom with danger.*
The Fox Who Served The Lion, p. 75

*Boasters brag most when they cannot be detected.*
The Fox and The Monkey, p. 73

*Deeds, not words.*
The Boasting Traveller, p. 27

*Do not attempt too much at once.*
The Boy and The Filberts, p. 27

*Do not count your chickens before they are hatched.*
The Milkmaid and Her Pail, p. 121

*Do not promise more than you can perform.*
The Imposter, p. 98

*Do not waste your pity on a scamp.*
The Flea and The Man, p. 64

*Equals make the best friends.*
The Two Pots, p. 176

*Every man for himself.*
The Three Tradesmen, p. 169

*Evil tendencies are early shown.*
The Blind Man and The Cub, p. 26

*Evil wishes, like fowls, come home to roost.*
The Bee and Jupiter, p. 23

*Example is better than precept.*
The Crab and His Mother, p. 40

*False confidence often leads to disaster.*
The Ass, The Cock, and The Lion, p. 13

*False faith may escape human punishment, but cannot escape the divine.*
The Eagle and The Fox, p. 52

*Give a wide berth to those who can do damage at a distance.*
The Archer and The Lion, p. 4

*Give assistance, not advice, in a crisis.*
The Boy Bathing, p. 29

*Greatness carries its own penalties.*
The Mice and The Weasels, p. 119

*Happy is he who learns from the misfortunes of others.*
The Lion, The Fox, and The Ass, p. 109

*He is no friend who plays double.*
The Hound and The Hare, p. 96

*If you are wise you won't be deceived by the innocent airs of those who you have once found to be dangerous.*
The Cat and The Mice, p. 35

*If you attempt what is beyond your power, your trouble will be wasted and you court not only misfortune but ridicule.*
The Eagle, The Jackdaw, and The Shepherd, p. 54

*If you choose bad companions no one will believe that you are anything but bad yourself.*
The Farmer and The Stork, p. 58

*You may change your habits, but not your nature.*
The Crow and The Swan, p. 43

*You may play a good card once too often.*
The Ass and His Burdens, p. 5

*You may punish a thief, but his bent remains.*
The Ant, p. 2

# List of Illustrations

**Illustrations used from the title page illustration**



**Half-Tone Illustrations**

Originally published as colour plates; these may viewed online at Gutenberg Project: <www.gutenberg.org/etext/11339>; or Wikipedia: <en.wikipedia.org/wiki/Arthur_Rackham>; Arthur Rackham and His Art: <www.bpib.com/illustrat/rackham.htm>.

## Black and White Illustrations

Photo: Arthur Rackham and His Art

# Arthur Rackham (1867-1939) was a prolific English book illustrator.

He was born in London one of 12 children. At the age of 18, he worked as a clerk at the Westminster Fire Office and began studying at the Lambeth School of Art. In 1892 he quit his clerk job and started working for *The Westminster Budget* as a reporter and illustrator. His first book illustrations were published in 1893. From then until his death he illustrated numerous books.

In 1903, he married Edyth Starkie, with whom he had one daughter, Barbara, in 1908. Rackham won a gold medal at the Milan International Exhibition in 1906 and another at the Barcelona International Exposition in 1911. His works were included in numerous exhibitions, including one at the Louvre in Paris in 1914. Arthur Rackham died of cancer in 1939 at his home in Limpsfield, Surrey.

Among the major works of Arthur Rackham children's books are *Fairy Tales of the Brothers Grimm* (1900), *Rip van Winkle* (1905), *Peter Pan in Kensington Gardens* (1906), and *Alice's Adventures in Wonderland* (1907), *The Wind in the Willows* (1908). He is best known for his elaborate children's literature illustrations, but he also illustrated books for adult readers: *A Midsummer Night's Dream* (1908), *Undine* (1909), *The Rhinegold and the Valkyrie* (1911) (also known as *Das Reingold*), as well as short stories by Edgar Allan Poe and several fairy tale books.

Rackham's artistic style of animal characterisation influences illustrators and animation artists even today. Note the similarity of Rackham's lion illustrations in The Fox and The Lion (page 72) to Scar (*The Lion King*), and Aslan (animated *Chronicles of Narnia*). Read more about Aurthur Rackham and his work online: <www.angelfire.com/ar/ArthurRackhamSociety>.

*Aesop*, by Diego Velázquez
c. 1639-40; Oil on canvas

# The Life of Aesop

The life and History of Aesop is very obscure. Sardis, the capital of Lydia; Samos, a Greek island; Mesembria, an ancient colony in Thrace; and Cotiaeum, the chief city of a province of Phrygia, contend for the distinction of being the birthplace of Aesop. Although the honor thus claimed cannot be definitely assigned to any one of these places, yet there are a few incidents, now generally accepted by scholars as established facts, relating to the birth, life, and death of Aesop.

He is, by an almost universal consent, believed to have been born about the year 620 B.C., and to have been by birth a slave. He was owned by two masters in succession, both inhabitants of Samos, Xanthus and Jadmon, the latter of whom gave him his liberty as a reward for his learning and wit. One of the privileges of a freedman in the ancient republics of Greece was the permission to take an active interest in public affairs; and Aesop, like the philosophers Phaedo, Menippus, and Epictetus in later times, raised himself from the indignity of a servile condition to a position of high renown.

In his desire alike to instruct and to be instructed, he travelled through many countries, and among others came to Sardis, the capital of the famous king of Lydia, the great patron, in that day, of learning and of learned men. He met at the court of Croesus with Solon, Thales, and other sages, and is related so to have pleased his royal master, by the part he took in the conversations held with these philosophers, that he applied to him an expression which has since passed into a proverb, "The Phrygian has spoken better than all."

On the invitation of Croesus he fixed his residence at Sardis, and was employed by that monarch in various difficult and delicate affairs of state. In his discharge of these commissions he visited the different petty republics of Greece. At one time he is found in Corinth, and at another in Athens, endeavouring, by the narration of some of his wise fables, to reconcile the inhabitants of those cities to the administration of their respective rulers Periander and Pisistratus.

One of these ambassadorial missions, undertaken at the command of Croesus, was the occasion of his death. Having been sent to Delphi with a large sum of gold for distribution among the citizens, he was so provoked at their covetousness that he refused to divide the money, and sent it back to his master. The Delphians, enraged at this treatment, accused him of impiety, and, in spite of his sacred character as ambassador, executed him as a public criminal. This cruel death of Aesop was not unavenged. The citizens of Delphi were visited with a series of calamities, until they made public reparation of their crime; and "The blood of Aesop" became a well-known adage, bearing witness to the truth that deeds of wrong would not pass unpunished.

Neither did the great fabulist lack posthumous honors; for a statue was erected to his memory at Athens, the work of Lysippus, one of the most famous of Greek sculptors.

These few facts are all that can be relied on with any degree of certainty, in reference to the birth, life, and death of Aesop. They were first brought to light after a patient search and diligent perusal of ancient authors, by a Frenchman, M. Claude Gaspard Bachet de Mezeriac, who declined the honor of being tutor to Louis XIII of France, from his desire to devote himself exclusively to literature. He published his *Life of Aesop*, Anno Domini 1632.

Excerpted from *Three Hundred Aesop's Fables*, translated from the Greek by George Fyler Townsend (George Routlage and Sons, 1867).